INTENSE LIES

A TRUE STORY OF THE INJUSTICE SYSTEM

TAREE BROWN

Praise for Taree Brown's *Intense Lies*

★★★★★ "You have to read it to believe it, but when you finish, perhaps, like me, you'll wish it were just fiction. Prepare yourself to be shocked by Tyler's story. He is a successful, law-abiding black man, a loving father, and a husband whose only crime was not knowing his second wife very well at all."

- Viga Boland for Reader's Favorite

"Brown is an articulate writer who, in Ty, has created a compelling character who struggles to fit together the pieces of an indecipherable puzzle."

- Kirkus Reviews

★★★★★ "A tragic tale that sheds light on the systemic racism and corruption embedded in America's judicial institutions, Intense Lies is as relevant as it is heartbreaking. Taree Brown's captivating story demonstrates perfectly how corrupt men in positions of power often abuse people and showcases the power of persistence and faith against all odds."

- Ammaarah Seboa for Reader's Favorite

New Lifeline Publishing LLC

Intense Lies: A True Story of the Injustice System

ISBN (paperback) 979-8-9858917-0-6
ISBN (ebook) 979-8-9858917-1-3

Cover design by Aaxel Author Services &
The Creative Studio by VeeVee
Interior design by Aaxel Author Services

Printed in the United States of America.

This book is dedicated to Cedric and Shaun Brown, my uncles who were like Big Brothers, who had a hand in the man I have become today. Rest in power.

ACKNOWLEDGMENTS

I must give special acknowledgment to the Creator of all creations for providing me with the strength to overcome the most difficult season of my life. I am also grateful to the many friends who encouraged me to write a book of this nature and supported me along the way. This book could not have been written and printed without the help of those people who gave their time and skills. I am indebted to my mother, Cynthia Brown, and grandmother, Bobbie Brown, for their constant support and encouragement; Nicole Johnson, for her support and willingness to fight a corrupt system with me; Alex and Nakita, for helping me evaluate and organize my first project; Nicki Richards, for her editing; Heather Cunningham, for her insight and support; Steven Dell; Dr. Hoffman, Dr. Salmansohn and Dr. Fisherman for their constant support when I wanted to give up.

CONTENTS

PROLOGUE

Typically, I'm not one for journaling. I don't like to sit inside my head like that. But when I found a dusty bundle of unopened index cards in the desk drawer of my hotel room, I felt compelled to write, to somehow make sense of these past few months where everything dear to me slipped through my fingers like a palmful of water. So, under the weight of my wife's abandonment, I tore the plastic off with my fingernail and began my journey backwards. I started the arduous task of facing the events like a good client in their first therapy session, replaying the ugly, dissecting the confusing, and completely agonizing over the what-if.

That's the hardest part because I still don't know what I did wrong. Despite hundreds of notecards now covered in scribbled memories, despite the pain in my wrist and the events organized before me, simplified in three-by-five blurbs, I'm still at a loss. After writing, ruminating, and scratching my head into sandpaper, I still can't figure out what the hell I did wrong. It seemed to me that there was little evidence of a grand moral crime on my part. I guess the universe was playing Russian Roulette… "We pick you," it said, and then everything came crashing down.

I'm a person of faith, so when I make a mistake, I own up to it. I acknowledge it and I apologize, both to God and to the recipient of my wrongdoings. But when you can't even identify your wrongdoings, how can you apologize? How can you correct a wrong that isn't even apparent? This is not like when you're driving and a cop flips on the lights and pulls you over, taking plenty of time walking over to you before asking, "Do you know why I pulled you over?" Is my taillight out? Didn't come to a complete stop at that sign? As a black man in a Southern state, I have plenty of reasons to be fearful and suspicious when I am stopped by the police. But at least there is some relief in being told what you did wrong, even if it seems minor.

That basic right, to be told what you are charged with, even if you disagree with it, seemed like a given, a basic rite you could rely upon. Now, I've discovered, basic rites are as flimsy as a three-by-five index card. So let me go back to when things were reasonable, when they made some sense...

SOMETHING'S OFF WITH CINDY

I can't remember how much time passed between my suspecting Cindy of seeing another man and the accident. But things had been weird ever since Cindy announced she no longer wanted to attend Sunday mass with Mom and me. For as long as I can remember, she'd always worked long hours at the hospital. As an OB-GYN, she had to do that sort of thing, put in lots of over-time and whatnot. But that never kept her from wanting to spend her Sundays at church. She loved going to church—the excuse to wear one of her florals, the exchanges with the regulars, the holy communion—but one day, her attitude changed. One day, she sat me on the bed, the one we picked out together at Sears on Fifth, and with an unfamiliar look in her eyes, she announced she didn't have time for it anymore. I stared into her pupils wrapped in amber. They were dancing around, evading my gaze, but I kept staring, searching for the woman who now appeared so distant in front of me.

Cindy was my second wife, and from the moment we shared our vows, at that very same church I frequent every Sunday, I knew I was marrying my soulmate. I made all my mistakes in my first marriage, but Cindy…she was my true life partner, and we built a comfortable life together. With her profession as an OB-GYN surgeon, and my business providing staff for nursing homes, our combined salaries provided us with everything we thought we would ever need. I can still remember the warmth in my chest when we signed the papers on our forever home. Our cheeks were aching because we couldn't stop smiling. If only forever was a sure thing.

In those early years together, we embraced our dichotomous lifestyles as successful money-makers during the week and total free spirits come weekends. We always went to the State Fair, even if it was raining. We'd go to the local bar and designate who was in charge of which chores based on a game of pool. And we'd assemble picnics just for the two of us by the lake, assorted cheeses and a sleeve of saltines, where we'd muse about life, God, all our mistakes and achievements. We never had children together, so we had the privilege of staying like newlyweds. No one was vying for our attention and stealing bits of our freedom. We could simply bask in each other's glow. We did have kids from our previous marriages, though—something that bonded us in those early days together.

One afternoon, when we were visiting Sedona, Arizona, we sat in the shade between two large standing rocks and wrapped ourselves in each other and kissed in the coolness and history of the rocks, and it felt so much like we were being healed, being joined together.

But then, Cindy reluctantly withdrew her lips, and she revealed her doubts about her family and the way they might have seen her.

"Ty, you know that I want to be not only a good doctor but a good mother too."

"I know that," I agreed. "I don't understand why you're filled with doubt about that. I've seen you with your kids. They love you. They've got no reason to complain." I paused, wondering whether that was so or not. "Or is there something you feel bad about and can't discuss with them?"

"No, no, they're great kids. But it's been a while since I got divorced. And at first, they'd ask, 'Mom, aren't you ever going to get married again?' And I'd try to reassure them that, 'Yes, one day, I'll find the right guy.' Then the years rolled by, and I didn't find anybody I wanted to be with. And my son and daughter, they just grew sadder. Their relationship with their own dad just dissolved into dust, and they needed a male figure. Just like you got that support from men even though your own dad took off."

I remember wincing when I heard Cindy remind me of that in Sedona. But she was right. I was fortunate.

"You don't doubt I love you, Cindy, do you?"

"No, I don't. And my kids know you love me too. And them. But I feel their judgment. Their insecurity. They look at me and I can see their disappointment."

I knew what she was asking of me. And I knew I didn't feel ready for it.

"I get what you're saying. To kids, time drags out forever. Waiting is so much harder for them than for us. And even so, you've waited a long time too, Cindy. But I'm just asking you to consider that it wasn't so long ago for me that Emily ended our marriage on a whim. It really felt like it came out of nowhere. And as much as that hurt, what really scared me was that Shaun might never be able to deal with it. And might even blame me. I think we're still solid, Shaun and I. But that happened not very long ago. My priorities are making both of you happy. I won't let this slide, Cindy. I promise you. I just don't want to get married for the wrong reasons. I have to know it's right."

I'll never forget the saddest and yet sweetest smile she gave me as she wrapped her arms around my neck, kissed me deeply and whispered in the dusty heat of the day, "Let's go back to our room."

The cottage we had rented was among a small grove of trees as you drove up into the mountains of Sedona. Sweat-stained and tired but very happy, we helped each other peel our clothes off and entered the beautiful, mosaic shower in the bathroom. The water and soap gently transformed the tension we went through during our picnic discussion about marriage. Cindy and I wrapped large, softly woven, golden towels around ourselves and made our way to the bed.

"I know for myself," she said quietly, her hands massaging my chest, "what I want for my children. But, Ty, I also know what I want for me. And what I want," she insisted, coming so close to me that her warm breath covered my lips before she even met them, "is you."

That time was nothing like how we had made love when we first dated. There were no stories, no fantasies, no role-playing. It was Cindy and me, being totally honest with one another. And I loved it. I decided then, since we could be this way with each other, that I wanted to get engaged. I couldn't risk losing her.

Really, it was so simple, so predictable, so normal for so long. Cindy and I had disagreements occasionally but never any major fights. Sometimes, she would start crying for no reason, and I would comfort her by placing both hands on her shoulders and whispering, "What's wrong?"

When this happened, she shook her head, dried her tears, assured me that I hadn't done anything, and simply stated, "Don't mind me. I'm just being silly." I could tell when she was lying, though, and I always wanted to push for more information in these moments. One time, I tried to do exactly that, which likely marked the beginning of the end of our marriage.

"Could you please just tell me what's wrong? I can tell you're thinking about something," I urged.

"No, no, I'm sorry…It's nothing, I promise."

"You always say that, but this is like the fourth time this month. What's going on? Is it something at work?" She played with the satin fabric tied delicately around her waist, fidgeting with the hem of it as she spoke. We were getting ready to visit a friend's baby shower when tears suddenly poured out of her. It was so much that she had to run back to the bathroom to fix her makeup. "Is it something with your family?" I continued to probe.

"No, my family's fine. Work is fine."

"So why did putting your shoes on cause you to cry? I don't get it. Was it something I said?"

"No. It's nothing you said. I don't know…"

"Well, you've been breaking down like this a lot lately, and I want you to know that I'm here for you. Whatever it is. You don't have to suffer alone. I'll carry the pain with you."

"Yeah…" A new tear welled in her eye before sliding down her cheek with a blink.

"Goddammit, Cindy, just say it! Let me in! This is driving me nuts!"

"I don't know! I'm just emotional, I guess! It might be hormones."

"That's bullshit!" My head was aching now, so I took a breath to fill it with oxygen. "I'm sorry. I don't mean to raise my voice. I meant it when I said that I'm here for you. I'm a pretty patient person, I think, and I want to prove to you that I'm here. It's just frustrating because I want to help you, but I don't know how." That's when she looked at me through slits, her eyes mutating under her fury.

"You can't help me, okay?! If I had an answer, I would have given it to you. I'm just upset! Can you just let me be upset?!"

We never talked about the things bothering her. I always wanted to, but Cindy would never budge. That was the last time I put pressure on her, but I was drowning in the unknown. That month was tough, but in general, her outbursts didn't happen often, and when they did, they left as quickly as they arrived like a cloud briefly blotting out the sun. So I let it go. I couldn't see the logic in relentlessly probing her, insisting on an explanation, when the rest of our marriage seemed perfectly secure.

But now, with my head pounding every day and with legal

problems beyond my understanding, I'm trying to find the moment when the ground beneath Cindy and me began to shake, leaving cracks too wide to straddle, the beginning moments of an earthquake neither of us could possibly sense was coming.

~

We found ourselves sitting on that bed about three months later, when she revealed she didn't want to go to church with me anymore. She had something important to tell me, she said. Although her tone and slumped shoulders made me pause, I was eager to hear what she had to say, eager she was finally ready to open up.

"Honey..." she began, taking both of my hands in hers, "I need you to understand. I love your mama, and I know church is important to you, but I just don't have enough time to myself. I need Sundays alone, whether it's going to a spa or just sitting by myself near some trees. You have to understand. It's nothing personal. This is just something I need right now."

At that point in our marriage, I didn't think we spent enough time together. Between our jobs and our other obligations, we were lucky if we sat at the same table for supper. But I didn't try to talk her out of it. I could tell she was feeling overwhelmed, and I agreed that Sundays she could have all to herself. When I conveyed the news to Mother the next time I picked her up for church, she put up a fuss.

"Where's Cindy?" she asked, as I swung the passenger door open. Normally, Mom sat in the back, but thanks to Cindy's absence, she'd now earned shotgun.

"Not coming."

"Oh? Why's that?" she probed dryly.

"She set some boundaries for herself. She says she needs Sundays for personal time."

"Personal time? It's the Lord's day."

"Well, maybe the Lord wants us to take care of ourselves from time to time, even on His holy day."

"That's nonsense. What's the real reason? You guys having problems?"

"No, Ma, we're not having problems. She's just overworked and wants to do something nice for herself on Sundays. It's been a while since you worked, but I'm sure you can remember how taxing it is."

"I worked on my feet forty hours a week and then took care of you on top of it. I never missed a Sunday mass."

"Well, times are different now, and I think Cindy deserves a day off," I defended. But the words sounded wrong as they left my lips. Did she need a day off? She mentioned wanting to go to the spa... but that's not something she ever wanted to do before. She didn't see the point in expensive manicures and facials. She called those things "frilly and frivolous." I'd have to check to see what her nails looked like when I saw her again this evening. I wondered if she would have to remove her wedding ring when she got her nails done.

"It's red!"

"Oh shit!" I pounded hard on the brakes, but I was already hovering over the lines of white paint, blocking the path for pedestrians. "Sorry, I guess I got distracted. Are you okay?"

"I'm fine, but you best be careful with me in the front seat here. Precious cargo."

"I know, Ma, I'm sorry." I tapped the gas gently when the light flickered green again.

Mom turned the radio dial down to level zero with an exhale.

"Look, I don't really care how Cindy chooses to spend her Sundays. I'd prefer she spend them in church, but only because I know that's what makes you happy. It just concerns me. What's more important than time with her family?"

"I don't know...I just know what she told me."

"I'd see what else you can find out. It just smells fishy to me, darling."

When Sunday evenings rolled around, I'd casually ask Cindy what she did. At first, Cindy told me about going shopping or dropping in on an old friend out of town or just having lunch by herself and driving her BMW with the top down through the countryside. But after a few weeks, she stopped indulging my questions. "Look, I just need Sundays to get away. I don't want to have to account for everything I do. It's *me time*. Can you understand that?"

The truth was that I felt a little hurt. Before all this, we told each other everything about where we went, what we did, and how we felt. My first wife, Emily, and I split up because she talked to her female friends and got the impression that I was controlling. Plus, we got married young, so when her friends convinced her she needed to have fun while she was still in her prime, we eventually split. Emily agreed with them, and I couldn't convince her otherwise. She grew distant and bitter, no matter what I did. So, finally, I gave in, feeling it was no use to persist any longer, upholding one half of an already severed marriage.

I was avoiding a confrontation with Cindy because I wanted our partnership to work. And Cindy's mood did seem to improve after she spent Sundays on her own. But she would sometimes go off to one of the bathrooms with her cell phone, whispering to someone on the other end at weird hours of the day. Most of the time, I could make out her voice but never the specific words she was saying. Obviously, it got me wondering who it was. Maybe she was innocently talking to a relative or an old friend about something personal, I thought. But I felt she should share those kinds of things with me. Anything she could tell her cousin, she could surely disclose to me. For a while, I repressed my concerns, switching the television on when I heard her echoes through the bathroom. But as the calls grew more consistent, so did my suspicions, until I decided I had to eavesdrop with more intention than I had used before.

One day, as I heard her slip into the bathroom and turn the shower on, I sat on the floor about five feet from the door. With my ear pointed in her direction, I balled my hands into fists and prepared for the worst while listening intently. First it was giggles, a light soprano of laughter that didn't sit right with a bathroom conversation. And it continued, more and more giggling, until I could finally make out some real words.

"No, he can't hear me," she whispered. My stomach constricted as I studied the woodgrain of our floorboards, streaks of beige and pine. I scooted closer. "He's asleep, I promise." *If only she knew…* "Oh *that's* why you wanted to know," she continued. *Wanted to know what? That I was sleeping?* "Well, I'm not wearing anything spectacular, not like I would if I were with you." Not like I would with *you?!*

My fists were now sponged with sweat. My breathing increased until I felt like one of those dogs during a nightmare, their stomachs rising and falling at a rate that appeared cartoonish. I could feel the blood rush to my head as I propped my knees, ready to get up and pound the door down. But the sound of her voice plopped me back against the wall. I had to keep listening.

"Tomorrow? I don't know…I think we better wait till Sunday," she cooed. *Sunday…*I repeated the word to myself like a crazed mantra. *Sunday. Sunday. Sunday.* That's it. She's been cheating on me. Whatever was keeping her busy on Sundays had to exist on the other end of that phone, and I wanted to pummel him into these floorboards I was sitting on. While everything inside of me wanted to kick the door down and scream at this person like I've never screamed before, a voice deep within me advised against it. *Just breathe,* I thought.

Think this over. Don't jump to conclusions. She's your wife and you made vows to one another. So I didn't confront her that night. Instead, wobbling to my feet like a drunk, I made my way back to bed and repeated my mantra till the sun peeked through the curtains… *Sunday. Sunday. Sunday.*

The following day, I decided I'd make my questions more blatant, more direct. "Who were you talking to?" I finally asked.

"Oh, just an old friend. Girl talk. You know."

I didn't know. I just felt jealous. Was she cheating on me with another man? Or was she just slowly but methodically extricating herself from me, sharing her deepest feelings with someone else, someone who definitely wasn't her husband? And then spending time with him doing God knows what every Sunday in the park.

That's when the accident happened. I heard the shower run, so I ran to the staircase, hoping to make it to the door with enough time to hear the greeting between Cindy and her mysterious companion. But my jacket got caught on the railing, so my tailbone hit the first step with a thud before the rest of my body toppled accordingly. I flopped like a grouper on a ship deck all the way down the stairs, screaming for help and wondering if it would come.

When I finally caught grip of one of the railing posts, I heaved for breath before yelling so loudly that the birds stopped chirping. *"Cindy!"* My head was mush, feeling light in some spots and heavy in others.

Speaking became a struggle after that, since words appeared like fireflies I could either work to catch or allow to float away with the breeze. I had bumps and bruises all over, and I couldn't remember simple things, like which toothbrush was mine, or whether we kept the sugar in the porcelain jar or the glass one in the cupboard. Instead of sleeping, I'd pretend to sleep while switching positions every ten to thirty minutes. One morning, I woke up with bags beneath my eyes, and they stayed there like a permanent fixture for the next six weeks. Eventually, I got put on meds. I practically begged the doctor, but when the pill finally wormed its way down my throat, I felt no different. It was rock bottom. I wasn't dead, but I didn't feel alive either.

Before the accident, Cindy at least bothered to keep up with her charade. She kissed my temples at night and smiled when the coffee pot dinged. But after the accident, her attitude shifted, and so did our dynamic. Instead of good night kisses and morning chatter, I got an angry wife, huffing into bed at one in the morning with an aggressive yanking of the sheets. Instead of pleasantries over coffee, I got door slams and glares through the mirror as she applied deodorant. I didn't imagine the accident would change anything really, but I could have never expected this. Our home that once contained the warmth of a fresh towel following a cool swim now felt as sterile as Cindy's work scrubs.

One evening, I attempted to forge that peace again. Despite my suspicions and my own dark feelings, I fixed Cindy her favorite meal—steak and potatoes, the little purple ones they only sold at the market fifteen minutes down the road. I set the table for dinner, but upon noticing the plate settings, Cindy just picked up her meal and remarked with a huff, "Jeopardy's on. I'd rather sit on the couch and eat this in front of the television." So we ate side by side, never exchanging a word.

She did pick up my prescription once, but other than that, there was little acknowledgment of the accident, let alone my physical condition. Even though she worked in a hospital, she never asked how I was doing. I asked her how her patients were doing, but she never once returned the gesture. Over time, her body language altered. Her light steps became heavy stomps, her ballerina posture became a wrestler's stalk. One time, she even entered the living room and upon noticing I was seated there, audibly grumbled, just to stomp in the opposite direction. She was done pretending. Clearly, she was entirely unempathetic about my pain. If anything, she was annoyed.

Immediately following the accident, Cindy had to go with me to the doctor because I sprained one ankle and broke my toe on the opposite foot. Needless to say, I was unable to drive. Before then, I had wondered if maybe I was wrong to imagine she was with another man. But when your wife or husband is in need, it sends an unsettling message to see your partner pull away, as if to say, "Your condition is making too many demands on me. Leave me out of it." Instead of joining me in the doctor's office, she'd ask to wait in the car where she'd sit for hours with the phone glued to her ear. I know because I peeked out the glass door more than once to check on her.

Everything was becoming unnervingly clear when I returned home from work about three weeks after the accident. I walked up to the front door, no longer needing crutches but still feeling wobbly from all the lingering pain. Then I jingled my keys in my hand until I found the home one—a sharp brass key, the largest one on my key ring. I wedged the gold point into the little hole with all my might, but it simply didn't fit. She couldn't have changed the locks, I thought. That was taking it too far. We hadn't even had a proper fight. But when I simultaneously banged on the door and rang the silicon bell like a manic DJ, I heard nothing on the other side. When I finally called the locksmith, they confirmed what I already assumed. The locks had been changed, and I was not given possession of the new keys. So I got in my car and punched the steering wheel without a second thought. Then I punched it again, and then again. My knuckles were red and throbbing, but the pain felt good somehow, necessary even.

I kept punching until I felt cold wetness on my cheeks. I couldn't hold back anymore. Slapping my head against the headrest, I wept. "Fuck you, Cindy!" I yelled between sobs, my arms shaking with energy I didn't know how to expend. With one final punch of the steering wheel, I breathed deeply. I had to move forward. I couldn't stay here forever, in this depressing, enveloping cloud. So I turned the key in the ignition and started looking for a hotel away from Cindy. The next morning, I'd think about all the things I didn't want to think about now, like if I needed a divorce lawyer, or how I was going to deal with the pending contracts with my healthcare company without the documents stored in my home. But for now, I'd grant my head some relief, still bumpy from the accident.

When I woke the next morning, my stomach spoke to me in an alien language, begging for food, so I stopped at the diner three blocks away for some waffles and scrambled eggs. I thought about calling Cindy, but I swear my headaches got worse every time the phone beeped just to end with Cindy's bubbly "I can't get to the phone right now..." So I sat in the booth and waited for my food in silence. The décor needed some sprucing up and the coffee tasted overly acidic, but the experience gave me enough energy to check in with Sabrina. Sabrina was my foster sister but also, conveniently, my office manager. She already knew how overwhelmed I was, since I'd sent her sporadic updates throughout the aftermath of the fall. I always found her voice soothing because it matched the slowness of my thoughts.

"How are you today?" she asked.

"I've been better...been worse," I replied honestly.

"Yeah..." Her voice trailed off. "So, she really changed the locks? Without a word?

"Not even a note?"

"Not even a note."

"What a bitch!"

"Ha! Yeah...I don't know...I loved her. I do love her. It's all so confusing."

"And you've had zero communication?"

"Pretty much. Not by my choice."

"God...Well, let me help you get settled in a hotel. Then we can look for an apartment. I can help out every step of the way. The kids are back in school now, so I have way too much time on my hands."

"Thanks, Sabrina. You're sweet."

"Oh, it's no biggie."

When I hung up the phone, I debated eating my last bit of eggs. Probably too cold now…I placed my napkin over my plate so the waitress knew to collect it. That's when a sheriff walked in through the side door. We made eye contact by accident, so I quickly averted my gaze to the stains on my coffee mug. But not a moment later, he was standing right in front of me. "Tyler Montgomery?"

"Yes?" I rasped, suddenly feeling very small wedged inside the little booth.

"These are for you." He placed a brown envelope next to my plate. "You've been served by the District of Cobb County. These are court papers with the details of your complaints enclosed. I suggest you look them over."

My eyebrows furrowed as I squeezed my lips together between my teeth. Papers? He reached for his hat and gave a sort of cowboy salute. I coughed slightly before finding my voice again. "But…what did I do? Are these divorce papers?"

He shrugged. "I'm just the messenger. Everything you need to know should be in that envelope. Good luck, sir." He sauntered out, and, in a flash, he was gone.

I peeled back the top portion of the envelope, wishing I could ask the waitress to discard it along with the remains of my breakfast. With a deep inhale, I slid the papers out and began reading the fine print. I was expecting some verbiage about divorce, but instead, I saw the words "restraining order." I also read Cindy's name. This had to be a mistake. Why would I need a restraining order? I had been kicked out of my own home.

Now the cogs in my mind were turning. I couldn't understand the words on this paper. Of course, I could understand *some* of them, but not enough to get any real answers. The term "restraining order" made the fresh food in my stomach jostle. Did Cindy file a restraining order? Even before she kicked me out of the house? And why would she do such a thing? What made her change her opinion of me so swiftly? And with such certainty? And why wouldn't she talk to me about it? One thing was clear...we weren't going to talk about it now.

I got in my car with the envelope wedged beneath my armpit. Sabrina sent a text with the directions to a nearby hotel, so I checked in at the lobby with nothing but a stack of papers and a few CDs I had in the glove compartment. Under the fluorescence of my temporary room, I paced the linoleum carpet, pondering my next move. After retrieving a phone book from the concierge, I made up a list of attorneys that handled both divorce and criminal complaints. Slowly but surely, they all refused to handle my case without telling me any useful information.

Then, I saw a lawyer listed on a separate piece of paper stuffed between some of the pages in the book. It was the guy one of my friends had mentioned a few months back. He was supposedly well connected with officials in the county. I debated whether to call him because I knew he was going to be plenty expensive, but with the way the rest of my calls went, it seemed I had no choice.

When I got Franklin on the phone, he sounded cheerful and confident. He even said he'd be happy to represent me.

"Let me call over to the DA's office," he volunteered. "I know everybody over there. We'll straighten this out. Can you come to my office at two-thirty?"

LOOKING GUILTY

If Franklin really was hooked into the court system, he should be able to find out what the charges were, or so I figured. But he wasn't the only established lawyer in Marietta. I didn't want to contemplate his hitting a roadblock as well. Then again, I was not naïve about justice. It was about money and power and like politics, about relationships and personal favors, as well as the law.

I got to Franklin's office building a little early, with a suit on. It was a modern three- story complex off of Marietta Square, on Park Square. The waiting room was elegant, understated. I was ushered into Franklin's office, with a wide picture window looking out across the historic downtown district.

Franklin was in his early fifties, with graying and thinning hair. He greeted me with a firm handshake and pointed to a chair. He looked down at some notes he had written, and I suddenly got the feeling that he was no longer very pleased to represent me. I did not know whether it was the color of my skin or what the district attorney's office had said to him. I felt the muscles tighten in my back and a dull pain creep into my forehead.

"Well, Tyler," Franklin began, his voice drained of friendliness, "you've got a complicated case here. I need to ask you some questions." He looked up and met my gaze. "And I'd appreciate your being completely honest with me."

This was not the beginning I was hoping for with him. "Of course."

"I talked to an ADA handling your case," Franklin said. "When we talked on the phone, you said you thought your wife had filed for divorce, but you also saw a restraining order?"

"Yes, I was hoping you could tell me exactly what charges were made by her?"

His voice deepened, for emphasis. "*Criminal* charges."

I swallowed whatever air was in my throat with a gulp. "I suspected my wife of cheating on me, but I didn't do anything to her. I didn't attack her or threaten her."

"What did you do that may have prompted her to file for divorce?"

I rattled off the same explanation I gave to the other lawyers who would not help me. "I believed that she asked to spend Sundays alone because she needed time away. But I heard her whispering to someone on the phone in the bathroom, hiding it from me."

"Whispering in the bathroom," he repeated, unimpressed.

"That's not all. I saw her car being driven by someone else while she was at work. I dropped by the hospital where she works. The car wasn't in her spot. I got her to come down and talk to me. I told her that I needed to borrow her car, in order to see what she'd say. And she started getting angry, told me she didn't have time to talk and left me there, without saying goodbye. Then, I got served this divorce summons the next day, the *very next day* at work. She had changed the locks on our house."

Franklin didn't look at all sympathetic. "You know she's charged you with stalking her."

"How can I be stalking my own wife?" I protested. "I just asked her about the car."

"At her place of work," Franklin added. "All right, let's put that aside for the moment. Was there any other behavior of yours that could be construed as criminal toward your wife?"

"Absolutely not. I want to know what the district attorney's office said specifically to you about a criminal charge."

Franklin paused and then sat straight up in his high-backed leather office chair, surveying me. "Tyler, I want to assure you that I have been practicing law in this county for twenty-one years. I know most of the judges, DAs, defense attorneys, hell, I know most of the secretaries in the Cobb County Courthouse. And I've never come up against a charge that made an ADA so damn angry that he nearly slammed the phone down on me."

"What did he say I'm being charged with?"

"He didn't. He wouldn't. He just said that you needed to surrender yourself to the sheriff's office."

The pain in my skull got worse. "Franklin, why should I surrender myself when I haven't done anything wrong and the DA won't even tell you what it is? What is going on here?"

"I just told you," Franklin said, some sharpness edging into his voice.

"Why can't you go over this guy's head and find out what the DA knows about this case? It's obviously a mistake, and they need to correct it."

"You think the DA made a mistake, charging you with a felony? That doesn't happen.

And if you don't mind my putting my cards on the table..." He waited for my reply.

"Yes, let's both be upfront about this." I waited.

Franklin lowered his voice and consulted his notes. "I've been told you're a flight risk."

"That's ridiculous," I replied. "A flight risk for suspecting my wife is cheating on me?

Which she probably is, and then she files for divorce against me!"

Franklin put up his hands, urging calm. "Look, I don't know that this criminal charge has anything to do with your divorce case. Let me ask you, what do you do for a living?"

"I have a business staffing nursing homes. I'm bonded and so are my employees, registered nurses, licensed practical nurses. We have to abide by a certain code of conduct to stay in business."

Franklin scratched his chin. "Well, I'm sure it has nothing to do with that." He leaned in toward me, his voice becoming softer, as if he were a priest trying to get a confession out of one of his parishioners. "Everything that's said here, Tyler, remains confidential, you understand. I want to do my best to help you. I need you to tell me if there is something maybe your wife found out about you, something that could be construed as illegal.

Something outside of your business."

I sighed, frustrated by the question. "Look, did you bother to ask about my background? I don't have a criminal record. I've never been arrested."

"And that's good," Franklin agreed, placating me like a child. "But clearly, you are going to need a criminal defense attorney for whatever this is about. And I've got to tell you, I can't help you fight this unless you come clean and tell me about it."

I threw my hands up in the air. We seemed to be getting nowhere. "Am I supposed to confess to something I didn't do?"

"No, no, we don't want that," Franklin quickly agreed. He leaned back in his chair, and neither one of us said anything for a while. Then, he tried a new approach on me. "Is it possible," he wondered aloud slowly, clearly wanting to choose his words carefully, "that your wife is involved with a criminal enterprise and has asked you to cover it up? Because even though a husband can't be compelled to testify against—"

"My wife is a doctor, a board-certified MD."

"I can tell you, Tyler, I've represented doctors who have written too many prescriptions, if you know what I mean."

"I don't think my wife is a criminal, but she overreacted when I confronted her about having an affair, and that's what the divorce is about."

"And you're sure none of your acquaintances have ever mentioned any schemes that are illegal to you?"

"Yes, I'm sure."

Again, we reached another impasse. Franklin looked down at the notes he had made.

He tapped a pen on the paper. Did he believe me? Did he think I was lying? I wondered if Franklin was calculating whether my money would be worth his involvement in a case neither of us could understand. He stopped tapping the pen and dropped it on the legal-sized notepad, almost as if he had made a decision. "You know, there could be another angle to this."

"What's that?" I asked, hopeful that he would provide a reasonable explanation.

"Okay, just hear me out. You hire nurses for these facilities. You do your best to make sure you hire reliable folks. But it's hard to be one hundred percent sure with all the folks you hire. What if one of those nurses did something, not to endanger a patient, but something else. Something illegal."

I thought a moment. It hadn't occurred to me that a nurse would be corruptible. It was unlikely but possible. "You mean, like stealing meds from the facility?"

"Yes!" Franklin responded energetically. "Or maybe a nurse stole something from a patient or staffer."

"If that was the case, why wouldn't they report it to me? I'd be the one to investigate it, to fire the person if guilty."

"Tyler, I don't want to upset you," Franklin said warily. "Yes, that would be one way of handling it. In fact, most might do it that way.

But what if the nursing home suspected the nurse and *you?*" He let that settle in my mind before continuing. "Hey, what if the nurse was caught and told them she was working a deal with you. Even if it's a lie—"

"It *is* a lie," I interrupted.

"Even if it is, that nurse might be cooperating with them, in order to get a lesser charge by blaming you."

While I didn't completely buy his scenario, Franklin had finally showed me that there were other possibilities I hadn't imagined.

"Well," I agreed, "I'm going to have to hire an attorney to defend me, no matter what the charge is."

"Uh-huh," was Franklin's clever reply.

"And how much is this going to cost me?"

"It's obviously a bit more complicated because the DA isn't going to reveal his hand until you surrender. I'd say it's a bit more than my normal retainer. Fifty thousand should cover it for now."

"Ow," I said.

"It's a criminal charge, a felony, whatever it is."

I shook my head. This was going to make a major dent in my bank account. "And what about handling the divorce?"

"I can't handle both cases. But I can recommend some attorneys who'll do a fine job for you."

I had to take action. Franklin was the last lawyer on my list in Cobb County. I figured going outside the county would mean using an outsider who was unfamiliar with local officials.

"All right," I decided. "I guess I have to pay to find out what exactly they're charging me with."

"I'm afraid so," Franklin agreed. "You'll just make it worse if they have to come after you."

"Speaking of money, how much is it going to cost me for the bail?"

Franklin looked confused. "Sorry, what?"

"The bail," I repeated. "How much will it be for a bail bond?"

"They didn't say."

"What do you mean? If it's a criminal charge, there has to be bail."

Franklin now looked suddenly uncomfortable. "Tyler, it looks like whatever is going on, they're hopping mad over there. They're not granting you bail."

"What are you talking about?" I said, my voice rising. The throbbing in my head increased. "You don't mention until the last moment that there's no damn bail, on a charge they won't explain? This is the United States of America, not some Third World country!" I angrily rose from the chair and Franklin stood a moment later.

"This is Cobb County, Georgia, Tyler. And I advise you to pay my retainer and surrender yourself to the sheriff. And then we'll see what's what."

"Like hell I will," I said, making my way to the door. "I don't know what they told you, but it sounds to me like you're more interested in taking my money than actually finding out what is going on."

I whipped his office door open, and it slammed against the wall. His assistant jumped at her desk. Franklin followed me out, now shouting, "The last thing you want to do is run from the law around here! It'll look for sure like you're guilty!"

I paused at his office door. "Guilty of what?" I demanded to know. And, not getting an answer, I stormed out.

MOTHER'S LOVE

By the time I got to my car after my failed visit with Franklin, my head hurt so badly that I didn't think I could drive safely. Out of my shoulder bag, I pulled out the pain medication that Dr. Warren, my psychiatrist, had prescribed for me.

After the fall, I first went to a medical doctor. I didn't have a general practitioner, since I hadn't needed to see a doctor for years. When I told the first doctor what had happened, his reaction was, "Really? It's remarkable that you're still alive."

It really bothered me. I didn't want his commentary. I wanted treatment for the pain. He suggested an over-the-counter remedy, and I told him I had already tried that and it didn't help.

He took an MRI and I suffered silently, waiting a few days for the results to come back. I had trouble reaching him that day on the phone and when he finally returned my second call, he announced, in a tone that sounded distant, removed from the whole process, "The results are negative. I don't see anything there."

"Well, what am I supposed to do about these blinding headaches?"

"I'm not clear on why you're having them. If you want a referral to a psychiatrist, I can recommend one."

I felt he just wanted to get rid of me rather than really explore the physical problem. So I agreed to visit Dr. Warren. With him, I hit the jackpot with pharmaceuticals, for pain, for anxiety, and for sleep. I figured that there was no drug he could prescribe that would clear my mind when it was foggy from the drugs.

I swallowed one of the pain pills without water, waiting for the ache to subside a little before starting my car. I didn't have my appointment with Warren for a few hours. I just needed to hear a voice that cared, that could comfort me.

I took out my cell phone and dialed. Sabrina answered. "Hi, Sabrina. I'm just checking in. How are things going?"

"Tyler, hi. Everything is fine here. How did it go with the lawyer?"

Just hearing her voice made me a little calmer. "I don't think he's going to help me," I said hesitantly. "He asked for more money than he told me on the phone. And he says I should surrender myself."

"Really?" I could tell she wanted to say more.

"Sabrina, I don't know. There's something so wrong with all of this. No bail."

"What?"

"Yeah. I found out after I almost turned myself in. It still doesn't make sense. No specific charge. It's like they've got the wrong guy and they don't want to check."

"Or admit it," she said.

There was a long pause, but it wasn't uncomfortable. I knew Sabrina wasn't going to pressure me to make a decision, even though I had to make one. It's one of the things I felt was extraordinary about her. She seemed to always know when I needed time to collect my thoughts. The drugs I had to take and the complication of the situation made it hard to come to decisions. Much like when we were kids, Sabrina never once asked, "So, what are you going to do?"

"I need to rest a bit before I see Dr. Warren again," I finally said. "I think I'll stop by Mom's place, talk with her a bit."

"That's a good idea," Sabrina agreed. There was another pause. "Your head's hurting, isn't it?"

"Yeah, well, after visiting a lawyer who just wanted my money, I guess it would." She laughed, and I chuckled along with her. "You drive carefully," she insisted.

"I will. The pill will kick in soon. I'll be all right." I closed my eyes and saw her face in my mind. "Thanks to you," I added, softly.

"We'll figure this out," Sabrina insisted. "Call me if you need anything."

"Thank you," I told her.

"Of course, Tyler," she replied.

My next call was to let my mother know I was heading her way. After I did, I started up the car. The head pain was still there but much more manageable. As I left the downtown area of Marietta, heading for the outskirts, my mind drifted to my childhood. Even though my father had left us when I was a baby, I had uncles and male cousins who had guided me, protected me, gave me life lessons, so that I wouldn't feel the loss of my father so deeply. I knew it was important that I had those male figures in my life as a kid.

But now, they were distant memories. My uncles had passed on. My male cousins had moved away, to go to college, fall in love, start families in other states. My love and appreciation for them hadn't diminished; we just grew apart, with time and distance. I didn't feel I could discuss my divorce from Cindy or the other charges with them.

I pulled up in front of my mother's simple, gray and white, two-bedroom home—the home where I was raised from birth. I turned off the engine and just sat in the car, my eyes closed. A series of random images from my early family life ran end to end. There was my mother's younger face, smiling so widely, watching me explore some of my toys on the small but well-tended lawn. The wooden train was my favorite, the way it left a patch of parallel dirt lines in its wake as I maneuvered it through the front yard. And I saw the memory of a birthday party for me with other neighborhood kids and some of their parents in attendance. Next, I saw my tire swing. I'd sneak out sometimes just to look at the stars as I rocked on that thing. That was when I'd thought I might have a future as an astronaut. Late at night, another time, my mother, exhausted from a day of work, still encouraged me as, defeated, I complained about the math assignment I couldn't figure out, no matter how hard I tried.

That's when I knew I *couldn't* be an astronaut. And then, in our living room, there I was, in my early teens, looking at a photo album, seeing my father posing, aloof, for a picture before I was born.

I heard my voice, asking my mother, "Why did he have to leave?" I didn't recall her reply. Maybe there was none. I forced my eyes open, ending the reminiscences.

How could I leave? The law would track me down. And there was the shame I would bring to my mother. But if I turned myself in, it was also a humiliation, the act of saying, in essence, "I am not guilty but everything is stacked against me, and I know there is little hope for now."

The arguments for and against running from Marietta spun around and around in my head. I wanted to walk into my mother's house and firmly and reasonably announce what I planned to do, and I felt weak because I couldn't decide.

Once inside, despite the predicament I was in, despite the lines of concern I saw lining her forehead, I felt the undeniable love there, and I just quietly sat at her kitchen table. She asked me three times if I was hungry, and I said no each time, smiling, trying not to think that this might be the last time I saw her outside of jail.

She wanted to help but didn't know how, and so she poured me some sweet tea. I made small talk, delaying as long as I could the news about no bail and no lawyers who were in a position to help, but finally, I had to reveal the information that I came to deliver.

"Mama..." I sighed. "I have to tell you something."

"Okay...what is it, honey?"

"It's...ugh..."

"Whatever it is, you can tell me," she encouraged. I stared into her eyes, brown and almond-like. Suddenly I saw myself as a boy again, hoping my struggles with math wouldn't disappoint her. This was far more severe. I so badly didn't want to crush her. "Just say it, Tyler."

"Well, a lot has happened in recent weeks. I got in an accident last month...three and a half weeks ago actually."

"An accident?! What kind of accident? The car looked fine when you pulled in..."

"No, no. Not that kind of accident. I fell down the stairs."

"Oh God, Holy Mary and Joseph."

"It's okay. It could've been worse."

"You have to be careful, Tyler!" Her eyebrows furrowed. She was using her serious voice, the same one she used when I accidentally stole a Twix from the grocery. I didn't even realize I had done it until she spotted my hand clutching it in the car. Boy, was she mad.

"I know, I know. I messed up my head pretty bad. I have these headaches that are constant, and there's no sign of them going away. But at least I can walk, you know? But there's more, actually."

"Oh boy," she sighed.

"This is the part that's really hard to talk about because...well, I'll just tell you." I inhaled deeply, glancing at her eyes for just a second before forcing my mouth to say the words out loud. "I think Cindy's cheating on me. She locked me out of the house, and she filed charges against me."

Mama slapped her mouth with her palm, her eyes as wide as I've ever seen. I could feel my shoulders tense up, but seconds later, they slumped with relief. It felt good to finally say it, even if the news was clearly upsetting. We sat in silence for a moment. I rubbed the handle of my teacup with my index finger, just so I had something to do until she finally broke the silence.

"I don't know what to say," she admitted.

"I know. I'm sure you have a lot of questions." I stared at my shoes as my voice wandered off. "I hope...I hope you're not disappointed in me. I want you to know that I've only tried to do the right thing."

"I know, honey. I could tell something was off. I know it's not your fault."

I smiled with just the corner of my mouth. Her support sent warmth through my body, just like the hot tea as it floated down to my digestive system.

"It's just so unfair," she moaned. "And now, with you having these headaches and all." She reached out and held my right hand in both of hers. I added my left, and we just sat there, with entwined fingers, silently fearing the worst.

"Mama," I finally said, "I want you to be proud of me and—"

"I am proud of you," she interrupted.

"I know. But listen. If I surrender myself, I'm surely going to jail with no bond and no attorney. If I run, well, they'll assume I'm guilty of something. But it would potentially give me time to find someone to represent me, maybe figure out what is actually going on with this case. But it matters a lot what you think." I waited for her reply. Her eyes were cast down.

Finally, she lifted her head. "Unless you've done wrong, and I'm sure you haven't, there's no decision you can make that will make me think anything less of you."

"Thank you, Mama," I sighed. "I know that, but it's so good to hear you say it."

"And since we're on the subject," she added, "if you need time to get out of town, to get a lawyer who will actually do something for you, well, I'll guarantee one thing."

"What's that?"

"If anybody from Cobb County comes sniffing around, I'll tell them, 'My son happens to be a grown man. What he does with his life is his own business, and I do not meddle.'"

"Perfect," I said. "I wonder if I can get you as a character witness in court."

"I'd be willing, but they'd probably say I'm too partial. Which I am." She smiled at me, and, for a moment, I felt as though everything was normal, like we were smiling over some tea, discussing Sunday's sermon at church, like everything was light and abundant, and Cindy was still my wife. I held on to that moment like a child holds on to a loose tooth.

~

The following day evaporated any peace I had previously felt. I had to take action now. I had to find answers. So I got in my car and headed toward one of my main locations for answer-scouting: Dr. Warren's office. His office was in the Governor's Ridge section of town. There were groups of three-story brick buildings with white trim and columns. Individually, any one of those buildings looked professional, even stately, but having a kind of business park with many of them, all looking the same, was strange to me.

I had been seeing Dr. Warren for just under two months. When I first asked him how long I should expect to come to his office, he asked me what I meant.

"I mean, usually, how long does a patient continue before there's enough improvement to stop?"

"Every patient is different," he answered, smirking slightly like he was amused.

"I understand," I said, "but is there an average amount of time a patient sees you?"

"It depends," he answered without answering.

The previous visits had been about obvious things, like the shock and pain of Cindy filing for divorce, the mixture of medications that were making me confused or sluggish, the fear I had about the charge that I could not understand.

But now, as I sat on the sofa in his office, facing him in his dark slacks, white shirt, tie and beige sweater, I wondered about the effect of not seeing him professionally, that is, if I went on the run. I was in the middle of talking about the distrust I had after what had gone on. He was nodding, indicating he heard me, and I was hit with the realization that I might not be able to tell him my plans. I knew there was such a thing as doctor-patient privilege, but did that extend to my possibly telling him I would be "unavailable" for a while? Wouldn't he ask where I was going? I'd have to make up an excuse. I lost track of what I was saying.

"Tyler?" Dr. Warren questioned. "You stopped suddenly. Is everything all right?" He sounded genuinely concerned. I blinked a few times. The AC was pumping air directly into my face. I had to lace my hands together to stop from shivering.

"I, uh, I forget sometimes what I'm doing or saying."

Dr. Warren looked down at his notes. "You feel like it is hard to trust anyone, between this unexplained charge and, of course, Cindy suddenly filing for divorce. Let's take one thing on at a time. I know it can be overwhelming. You'll learn more later about the county charge. Let's get some more perspective about what may have happened between you and Cindy." He leaned in toward me, his pen upright in his hand, resembling a curious detective.

"Okay. Where do we start?"

"Let's go back to when you first suspected her of having an affair. You said you would sometimes hear her whispering into her phone while in the bathroom."

"Right."

"But you've also said that you never heard what she said, and so you couldn't be sure of who she was talking to."

"Wait," I said. I closed my eyes, trying to recall our previous session. "I did tell you that I heard a bit of one of those phone calls."

Dr. Warren sat up in his padded chair and pursed his lips. "Tyler, actually I don't think you did mention it."

"I'm sure I did," I protested.

"No, I would have made a note of it. Perhaps you meant to bring it up but we ran out of time."

I shook my head. "The medications. They're confusing me. Can we figure out a better dosage for all three of them?"

"Yes, of course, but let's stay on this conversation you heard on the other side of the bathroom door." His eyebrows turned inward as he stared into my pupils.

"Well, she had been going off on her own on Sundays. I complained. She said—I heard just a part of it—but I heard her whisper into the phone, 'I can't see you this Sunday.'"

"And that's all you heard?" He questioned while scribbling onto his notepad, looking up to catch my gaze as he continued writing.

"Yes."

"Tyler, let me remind you that when Cindy wanted more time to herself, you agreed," he remarked. His voice carried the same authority as my father's when I got all those ant bites. *I told you not to go out barefoot.*

"Yeah, but I didn't want to," I protested. "I did it to make her happy."

"Right," Dr. Warren said. "Then, you pressured her to find out how she spent her Sundays. And it was after that time that Cindy made private calls when she thought you weren't nearby."

I waited for the doctor to say something more. After a long pause, he said, "I'm sorry. Reliving that moment must have been painful."

"Yeah," I answered. "And what kind of person files for divorce instead of talking out problems? Unless she saw I was on to her and she decided to file first."

"Tyler, if you and Cindy would have tried to talk things out, what do you think would have happened?"

"I don't know. I don't think she wanted to talk it out. She just wanted to leave."

"I know. But if you both had talked about it, gone to couples therapy, and you found out that she had gone outside the marriage, would you have forgiven her?"

That made me stop short. "If she never filed against me?"

"Yes."

"Never locked me out?"

"Right."

"I would have tried to work it out. But it's too late now."

"Tyler, I have seen couples go through absolutely horrible times and still come back together. If there is the ability to forgive on both sides, anything is possible."

"Yeah, well, if she isn't willing to take my calls, I don't know what I can do."

"We'll explore that next time, okay?"

"Okay." I still hadn't decided what to do about leaving town, and that meant I might not see him for another session. I decided to keep my options open without telling him anything definitive.

We both stood up and I started for the door.

"By the way," he asked casually, "have you talked to Sabrina and other family about what's going on with all this?"

"Sabrina? She knows basically what's up."

"But you haven't discussed anything in detail with her, then?"

"No."

"Okay, let's also discuss this further next week. Call me if you have any issues with your medications."

"Thank you," I said, and then I walked out.

RETURNING TO THE SCENE

When you visit your psychiatrist, you're supposed to, ideally, feel free to be completely open about your problems, not wonder if he or she is going to report your plans to the police or doubt what you say is the truth.

But that's exactly how I felt about Dr. Warren as I left his office and drove toward mine. His statement about our need to talk about Sabrina was puzzling because she had kept my business running and my spirits up during the physical and emotional crisis. I was fond of Sabrina, and she filled the role of a trustworthy sibling that I'd lacked for a long time growing up.

And as I walked up the stairway to the second floor of the office building for my staffing company, there she was, on the phone, a folder open, checking papers and double-checking them against a computer screen. Even with all of that distraction, Sabrina instantly turned to me as I opened the door. Her smile warmed me, and I knew how much harder my life would be, how much more insurmountable the predicament would seem, if I didn't have her with me.

I waved and sat down at my desk, checking voicemails and

seeing if there were any outstanding emails that had to be addressed. In typical fashion, though, she had it all under control. I didn't have to make any major decisions about workflow. Instead, I thought of the people in my life who meant the most to me, people I hated the idea of being separated from for an extended period of time: my mother, Shaun, Sabrina.

"How did it go with Dr. Warren?" Sabrina asked after she'd finished her call. She was smiling, but her expression of support melted away when she saw me uncap a bottle of pain pills. "Not so great, then?" she guessed.

I chuckled a little, if for no other reason than to give her a little reassurance. I didn't want her to worry about me, but she already was, and I had a responsibility to be honest with her. She sauntered over to my desk and sat on the edge of it.

"He's concerned," I insisted, "but sometimes my head hurts a little more after talking to him."

"I'm just as concerned as he is," she said softly, her big-sister instinct kicking in. "Can I get you some coffee or anything?"

I wondered how I was going to break the news about my leaving. It was hard to guess her reaction. Would she support my decision to flee? And if she didn't, what would that mean? I'd already made up my mind. I couldn't change it now. Still, the pounding in my head grew more intense whenever I seriously thought about boarding the plane to West Palm.

Could I even be certain this was the right decision? My palms suddenly felt sticky with sweat.

"I think you're going to want some of these pills," I tried to joke. It fell flat. Her lips parted, her concern silent but very clear.

"What are you thinking?" she demanded to know.

I got up and poured myself a Styrofoam cup of water to take my pills. It gave me the space to get as serious as I could about her.

"No matter what I do, Sabrina, I'm going to take care of you.

As long as I have a job, you have a job. Even if I'm not around, I'm going to know what's going on with you, personally. Not just how the company is running, but how *you* are. I'm going to help you in every way I can. I need you to know that."

"I'm not sure what you're saying. Are you going to shut down the business?"

"I'm going to avoid it at all costs. But not a single lawyer will help me, and not one can tell me how I can be charged with a felony that they won't describe and without bail."

Sabrina shook her head of dark curls, as if the motion would somehow help the last sentence make sense. "It *has* to have a bail."

"I'm being framed by someone, and I don't know how to find out more."

Sabrina interlaced her fingers and squeezed them hard together. "Is it Cindy? Is she doing this to you because you caught her?"

"I think it's obvious she instantly filed the papers because of someone she is with. But really, this whole felony thing has to be a clerical error. It doesn't make any sense."

"Believe me," she insisted, "I haven't filed anything wrong. I haven't gotten any notices or warnings or—"

I smiled and held a hand up to stop her. "Please, I'm lucky to have you. This isn't about you doing anything wrong. In fact, it's about how important you are."

She took a breath and smiled. "Okay, then. By all means, tell me how important I am."

I pulled up a chair for her so we were looking at each other on the same level, as equals. "On a normal day," I started, trying hard to get the words right despite the fogginess in my head, "there's so much I want to tell you. And today, I have to make some quick decisions, and I wish I had more time."

"More time for what?"

"I'm leaning in the direction of leaving town, staying with a friend in West Palm Beach. There is already an arrest warrant. That is why they want me to turn myself in."

I wanted her to say, "I understand. I'll back you up in any way I can," but the words that came from her were a struggle to say, and I couldn't fault her.

"Tyler, wait. Think for a minute. If you run, it will hurt your case even more. They'll assume you're guilty, even if it is just a stupid office error."

"You're right, but at the same time, if they throw me in jail without bail, I could be there for a long time with no way to get the right legal representation."

I let that sit with her for a while. She didn't come back with an immediate reply. She knew this was a tough call. Smart woman, Sabrina.

"So," Sabrina began slowly, sounding out a plan, "you go to your friend, you don't tell me where exactly you are, but you check in. If the cops show up here, I tell them something like you are on a business trip and I don't have any more information. Just because you're like my brother doesn't mean you tell me anything."

"Perfectly said," I replied. "I want to minimize your involvement if it goes down that way."

"I am involved!" she said with an edge of hurt that surprised me. "You're my little brother. I can't just flip a switch and not worry about you going to prison. If they make this bullshit charge stick, it could be years and years and—"

I held up my hand again to stop her, but this time, the thickness in her voice and the moisture in her eyes did the job. I bit down hard on the inside of my lower lip. Then I took her two slightly shaking hands in mine.

"Sabrina, there is not a thing I have ever asked of you that you didn't do perfectly for me.

Nothing would make me happier than to get rid of this stuff

hanging over my head." That got her attention.

"It's going to be very difficult for a while. They're closing down the business until this gets straightened out. I have to be away from Marietta for now. I wish I could resolve this right away. But soon, we'll figure this out. I promise. If the cops visit you at home, you call me."

"You think I'm afraid of some cops hassling me?" she replied angrily. "You know how many times I had white cops hassle me since I was in high school, making sexist remarks, asking for my ID for no reason? I can handle them six times a week and five times on Sunday."

"I know you can," I agreed softly, thinking about some of the things she'd dealt with when we were teenagers. "Try not to worry. You're on the payroll, and nothing is going to change there."

"You think I'm worried about you stiffing me on my salary?"

"I'll tell you right now, Sabrina. I will go without eating before I stop paying you."

"Don't do that," she said. "But I'm getting a raise after all this is over."

It felt good to laugh, even a little.

"I assume you haven't told dear Dr. Warren about your travel plans?" she asked as we both stood up.

"You know," I said, "you ask all the questions before I can even tell you. I'm telling him nothing about West Palm. I may go back for a last visit though. Is there any message you want me to give him from you?"

"Yeah, if he makes your life one percent harder, I will drive over there and kick his ass around the block."

"I may put that in my own words, if that's okay." I moved to her and extended my arms. "Call you later."

"I know," she said, but it was barely audible, more like mist than words.

~

Living in an apartment after having the home you shared for years with your ex-wife and son is an act of adaptation. It wasn't a bad place. The neighbors weren't rude or noisy. It was a one bedroom but with a good-sized living room. But of course, it didn't feel like a home. It was the best available option in Marietta when Cindy locked me out.

It was unfurnished, and to save time and deal with the other issues that had been dumped on me, I simply rented furniture to fill it rather than buying anything. I did purchase dishes and glassware and cooking utensils, but after dealing with the attorneys, my business, the doctors and physical pain, I was in no mood to come home to an empty kitchen and start whipping up some veal scallopini.

I was a confirmed bachelor again. My lack of cooking skills meant that I'd come home at night and put on some music to drive the loneliness and fear out of my head, while the new, clean and unfamiliar kitchen I now used became the laboratory for less-than-gourmet meals. I dabbled in experimental pasta and meat sauce, egg dishes with vegetables diced into them or, on my roughest days, when the energy was not there, something frozen that looked good in the freezer section but was eventually bland when it reached my tongue.

I was allowed back into the house three days ago, just to get essentials only. There were no other cars when I pulled into the driveway, which is exactly what I'd anticipated. Even so, I couldn't help but plop my head against the steering wheel upon putting the car in park. I wasn't ready to walk in yet. My head was pounding harder than ever, and I was too lazy to grab more pills. When I lifted my eyes again, I took in the scenery before me.

Everything looked the same, same dead plant hanging next to the garage, same door handle—gold and glistening in the sunlight—same cobblestone walkway mosaiced across the lawn. For just a moment, I could imagine that nothing had changed. I could imagine I had just returned from work, eager to taste Cindy's stew. But I didn't let myself fantasize for long; it would be too painful. I was here under different circumstances now. And as much as I stared at the front window, hoping to catch a glimpse of the wife I once knew, I knew I was only making myself suffer. I had to choose to stay in reality.

With a deep breath, I opened my car door and walked down the cobblestone, determined. This only had to be as painful as I allowed it to be. That's something my therapist would say. My hand trembled as I reached for the doorknob, but I yanked it open as if to gain power over it. This was my house. I painted the walls and mowed this lawn like it was a sacred ritual. I could retrieve my things without breaking down. Or at least, that's what I told myself.

Upon entering, I didn't dilly-dally. Instead of absorbing the atmosphere and looking to identify any changes, I dashed straight to the bathroom. Under the sink was my little black toiletries pouch. I pinched its nylon fabric with my fingers and began filling it with whatever I could find: deodorant, toothbrush, razor, shampoo. I sighed with relief as I zipped it shut.

That wasn't so bad. Next stop, the bedroom. I made quick steps, trying to keep my momentum going. But as I walked over the floorboards leading into the master, I paused at the familiar squeak from the wonky board beneath me. I guess Cindy's new boyfriend didn't care to fix it either. The bag of toiletries felt moist in my grip. I had to get this over with.

Sliding the closet door with one swift motion, I grabbed my duffle and started piling clothes inside, hangers and all. I threw my underwear on top, a heap of bundled fabric. Then, with a quick scan, I hurled the bag over my shoulder and stomped to the front door. I stared at the knob for a second before my arm moved to grab it. Did I need anything else? Did I *want* anything else? Any semblance of closure from this surreal visit? A visit to my own home?

What a bizarre scenario…

I walked into the living room for a moment, just to see how it would make me feel. There was a new blanket strewn over the sofa. I picked it up and rubbed the fleece between my fingers. Holding it up against my nostrils, I let the scent waft over me. It didn't smell like Cindy. It smelled like something unfamiliar, something musky. My throat started to tickle as I released the fabric with a cough. It was time to get out of here. But first, I needed to check my home office. I scanned the room for a minute, but there was nothing I would need, just some half-used notepads and stacks of printer paper. I wondered if there was anything in Cindy's office. I knew she kept some belongings of Shaun's in there.

As much as my life had been turned upside down, I wasn't there to exact revenge, especially when it came to her stepson. I had my laptops and a number of flash drives with photos on them already in the trunk of my car. I would eventually, when I felt strong enough, go through them, deleting many images of Cindy but keeping others I was strong enough to look at again.

But as I stood alone in Cindy's office, at her desk, I saw that she had a number of framed photos of Shaun, just by himself. In one, he stood smiling, about nine, in his Little League uniform, a bat resting casually over his shoulder. In another, he hung upside down on a jungle gym in the local park, his mouth open with unrestrained joy.

A third snapshot on the desk was Shaun in his room, and I remembered taking it. He had been doing his math homework at his desk, and I was stretched out, my legs hanging well over the edge of his small bed, reading an essay he had written about Native Americans and the first Thanksgiving in the colonies. I remember there was a sentence in his essay, which was due the next day. It read, "What was special about the Native Americans and the colonists having the first Thanksgiving together was that the land belonged to one group of people, and they still welcomed others from far away. It made them all citizens together, even though they were so different from each other."

I had read the words silently to myself and cleared my throat. Shaun had looked up from his math, concerned. Then, I slowly, carefully, respectfully read his words aloud.

"Is it okay?" he asked.

"Nope," I said, casually, lightly, so he wouldn't be alarmed. "It's a lot more than okay.

It's perfect."

He got a crooked grin on his face, one that said I was embarrassing him with too much praise but praise that at the same time he loved. He went back to work on math, his pencil dipping up and down, while I gently rose, pulled out my cell phone and took a picture of him deep in thought.

I had made a color print of it, and Cindy loved it so much, she framed it and put it on her desk here. I stared at that photo and noticed my eyes getting moist. I thought to myself, *Cindy, when you decided to give up on our marriage, you also gave up on both of us raising Shaun together, just like Emily gave up*. And I was not proud of what I did next. I removed the shots of Shaun, all three, from the chrome and copper picture frames and stuck them in my jacket pocket to take back to the hotel. I already had digital copies of them. I didn't want the frames. I wanted Cindy to come home, see the empty frames, know that I had taken the pictures with me and remember that her refusal to try and save our marriage was also her decision to avoid whatever damage it might cause my son. I was more upset about her giving up on him.

As I looked once more at the now empty picture frames, I thought about how we never got a chance to formally tell Shaun about the divorce. Hell, it was a surprise to me too. I remember when he called just the other day, asking if he could stop by to pick up one of his books. My voice cracked as I tried to explain the situation. I didn't want to drop such a massive bomb over the phone, so I just lied and said the house was getting fumigated for termites, but he could sense the turmoil in my voice. He kept saying, "Dad? Are you sure everything's okay?"

"Yeah," I replied, trying to convince myself everything was okay just as much as I was trying to convince him. "Let's get dinner sometime next week and we can catch up," I told him.

I still haven't broken the news. Telling my mom was hard enough; I could wait a little longer to tell Shaun. This house visit was enough intensity for a while. I needed to get back to the hotel to clear my mind.

With one final glance, I whispered goodbye to my old self, and then marched to the car without looking back. With the keys in the ignition, I glanced once more at the view in front of me. This image used to feel like the pop of an umbrella in the midst of a rainstorm, safe and warm. But now, it just felt foreign, like a building I drew up in a dream. I reversed until the house was next to me. Then, with a final squint through the glare of the sunlight, I drove away forever.

Driving always put me in a meditative state. I couldn't help but reflect, as much as I wished I could think about anything else. I was not only furious that Cindy had brought our marriage to an end so abruptly but also disgusted with myself that I had not found a way to get some resolution, some understanding from her. It's one thing when a couple has a trial separation. There is some dim possibility that, through therapy or making private time for real honesty with each other, you can somehow inch your way back into each other's lives, find forgiveness, begin again, do better.

Even as the years go on and stretch endlessly with no sense of reunion, in rare moments, there is still a bubble in time, when two people who were very much in love have the space in their lives and can, with caution, even with fear, reach out their hands to each other again. That, I sadly felt, had been damned as a possibility by my ex-wife. And yet, after I had loaded up the car with just things I owned, a small part of me was not ready to leave. It was so quiet sitting alone in our home, Cindy purposely gone, Shaun still in school, but something held me there longer. I didn't want to admit my family life was a failure. Walking out the door was the final admission of that.

But it was something else too. And I wanted to explore it, which I decided to do when I arrived back at the hotel.

After the key card made the door handle blink green, I opened the heavy door leading into my new and temporary home. Immediately, I put a frozen lasagna in the microwave, even before I took off my shoes. Then, I went through the large, thick stack of rubber-banded notecards I had collected ever since the accident. They now contained writing on every inch of them, dated notes about moments in my life. When I first started my index card diary, I didn't think much of it in terms of record keeping. I just knew I had to get all my thoughts down, to make sense of these past few months when life went from comfortable and predictable to utterly confusing and uncontrollable. But over the past few days, I'd made a habit out of reading and re-reading all my notes, every morning and every night like a personal bible. So, after retrieving my lasagna, hot to the touch, I carefully held the fork that dipped into the microwaved spinach lasagna, while using my other hand to flip through the beginning days of my three-by-five journal.

It didn't take long to find my most recent card, sitting right there on top, the exact card that brought back the moment. Although I wrote it just a few hours ago, it felt like yesterday at this point. My lettering was in block print, a little sloppier than normal, due to the emotion of it all, but clearly legible.

"ALONE ON COUCH BEFORE LEAVING HOUSE FOR THE LAST TIME. WHAT AM I LEAVING BEHIND THAT I DESERVE AND NEED TO TAKE?"

There was no answer on that card. But I knew what it was. I let my fork drop into the no-longer-warm red sauce, covered my eyes with both hands and went back in my mind.

Just yesterday, I had sent an email to my old friend Ron in West Palm, letting him know I was going to call last night. I tidied up the kitchen, opened the refrigerator, stared at the food, realized that I was just numb and distracted and not hungry and closed the door. It was not late, near 6:30, and I figured Ron would have already been home for an hour.

I got him on the third ring. His deep voice was strong, welcoming, and it felt so good to hear. I had previously told him that Cindy and I were divorced, but he didn't know the rest. As one of my oldest friends, I planned to tell him, but it had to be in person and it had to be gradual, to give him a chance to absorb a huge amount of information. I knew that I would listen very carefully to his advice on my situation when I was finished explaining, but giving someone too much information too soon doesn't help them come to a good decision. Unless, of course, the person is finally being told why he's under indictment.

"You're still coming, I hope," Ron began.

"Oh, yeah," I assured him. "I can't wait to see you."

"A couple of old schoolmates out on the town again. I can get my girlfriend to bring along someone for dinner if you want."

"That's nice of you," I hesitated, "but when I get there, I'm taking you to your favorite restaurant and it's just going to be the two of us."

"All right by me. Hey, how you doing, for real? I'm sorry about you and Cindy."

"Thanks. It's going to be all right." I thought about the irony of the next thing I said.

"I've got a lot of news to share. And I want to hear all about you."

"Well, I got the condo all to myself. Anna has her own place, so you can stay here as long as you like and have plenty of privacy."

"Oh, thank you. I'll just be staying a couple of days," I informed him, "but it's going to be great. I have some business to take care of tomorrow, so I was thinking of getting there the day after. Does that work?"

"Absolutely."

That call had given me a small rise in energy and focus. It was still before seven o'clock. I wanted to accomplish a lot my last day in Marietta. I opened my contacts menu on my cell phone and dialed my first wife, Emily.

"Hello, Tyler," she said with a kind of exhaustion in her voice that suggested we had talked seven times that day, rather than a week ago.

"Hi, Emily. Listen, sorry to call at the last minute, but I have to go out of town on some business for a few days and won't be able to see Shaun like I normally do. Would it be okay to come over just for like a half hour, chat with him and then be on my way?"

Emily was not usually open to changing my regular visits. There was a long pause. "I wouldn't be seeing him for another week," I gently added. "I promise. A half hour and I'm gone."

"Let me talk to him. He's in his room. Hold on."

I closed my eyes and hoped, listening. Finally, Emily came back on her phone. "Can you come over right now? He's doing homework. I don't want him up late."

"Of course," I said, "on my way. Be right there. Thanks, Em." The rush of words poured out, and I hung up before she even had time to say goodbye, assuming that she did.

I grabbed my jacket and car keys, and then a disturbing thought came to me. If the Cobb County DA found me on the run or caught up with me even after I returned from Palm Beach, the visit with Shaun might be the last time we saw each other when I was not in jail. All I'd have is thirty minutes and what could I actually tell him about my life, about his, under the circumstances?

I wasn't about to inform Emily of my exact itinerary in West

Palm, either. I couldn't rely on her keeping information private if the police or court asked her about me. I didn't want Shaun involved at all in any of this, if I could manage it. So it was about protecting me and those I cared about too.

I flipped on the outside light and left the apartment, locking it, and headed toward the car.

Who else did I need to contact? Dr. Warren came to mind. He was expecting to hear from me, and if I just disappeared without making a follow-up appointment, that would be enough for him to contact the authorities.

It was just after seven. I started the car and dialed Warren's cell phone, expecting to leave a message.

I was pleasantly surprised when he picked up, although his greeting was abrupt. "Tyler, what's going on? Are you okay? Is this an emergency?"

I knew he had to ask me that. "Doctor, thanks for taking the call. It's not an emergency, but it's important. I'm sorry to call late in the day."

"What is it?"

I don't like lying and I'm not sure I'm any good at it. But for my own safety, I had to convince Dr. Warren what I was about to say was the truth. And his living was figuring out when people were lying to themselves and others.

"I thought we had a really good session today, and I had some new thoughts to share with you. I know you're busy, but is there any way I could come in tomorrow? Any time, early, late, whatever you've got."

There was a pause on his end and I looked at my watch, thinking I needed to start driving to see Shaun.

"Well," Dr. Warren drawled, taking even more time, making me anxious, "I'm certainly glad that you're having some insights. I look forward to hearing them. Let me discuss this with my assistant tomorrow, and we'll find a time to fit you in. She'll call you in the morning."

"That is great. Thank you."

"Absolutely, glad to help."

"I'm looking forward to getting the call tomorrow morning and seeing you. Thanks so much, Doctor, and goodnight."

I hung up before he could say another word. It felt good. I put my car into drive and squealed away from the curve, trying to formulate what I would say to my son.

NOW DIVORCED

I generally found some time, each weekday, to spend with him. It wasn't in huge blocks of time, but it might be picking him up from school or meeting him at a diner for a snack in town as he made his way home. I stayed out of Emily's way on the weekends so she and Shaun wouldn't feel crowded by me, but today, I had to make a visit to talk to her.

Emily opened her front door, leaning on the frame, as if she was not ready to make up her mind to let me in.

"Come on in," Emily said, more a groan than an invitation. I don't think her attitude would have improved if she knew the jeopardy I was in. But I wished for this visit to be calm, to be something that would serve as a good memory, at least for Shaun, if things went badly for me in the future.

I eased inside the small, two-bedroom house and thanked her. I sniffed the air and smelled the lingering odor of their meal.

"I hope you're all done with dinner," I offered. "I don't want to interrupt."

"No, no," she protested softly, "your timing's okay, I guess. We ate. He's in his bedroom, doing homework." I nodded my thanks, but she was clearly curious. "Didn't you already see him at the park today? You don't usually see him twice in one day. Is everything all right?"

"Oh, sure," I said, hearing my voice rise a little unnaturally in an effort to convince her. "I have to go out of town, but it's for a good reason. I'm expanding the business."

"Expanding?" she asked, cocking her head doubtfully.

"Yeah, I found some new potential nursing homes that look like good chances."

"And where would these be?"

I really didn't want to dive into a discussion, so I decided to just keep it simple. "Florida. Heading out there for a few days, have some meetings."

"You planning to move out of state, Tyler?" she asked.

"I'm very happy to be here in Marietta and be an important part of Shaun's life, so, no, you don't have to worry about that."

"So what town are you visiting?" she asked, and I felt the muscles in the small of my back tense up.

"Listen, let me chat with Shaun a little. He can finish up his work, and we'll talk on my way out. Is that okay?"

"Whatever," she said, moving off casually without even looking back, finally letting me walk down the hallway to Shaun's room. I got to his door, knocked gently and waited.

He opened it. "Hey." A shy smile was waiting for me.

"How about a break from homework? Unless you're having such a great time doing it, and then, I don't want to interrupt."

"No problem," Shaun said. "Come on in."

I thought about it a moment. "Let's sit outside on the back patio. Spring is here. It's not too windy."

The house had a modest back lawn and picnic table with an umbrella for shade. We made ourselves comfortable there.

"What did I take you away from?" I asked.

"Right now? Math. Feel free to interrupt me any time I'm doing math."

"You're doing great at all your subjects," I volunteered.

"Yeah, but some take a lot more work than others." He paused, looking a little uncomfortable. "Did I overhear you say you're going out of town? You didn't mention anything about it earlier."

It bothered me, not telling Emily the full story, and it was going to upset me even more not to be able to tell him, but you do what you have to do to protect your family the best that you can. I quickly gave him the summary about looking into additional work in Florida.

His eyes narrowed with concern. "You're not going to have to move there, are you?"

I felt a twinge of pain in my chest, seeing his expression of worry. "No way. But hey, if I can help the business grow, I'd be crazy to pass on it." He nodded and sighed a little. "So, since it is, in fact, spring now," I brought up, "can you find time to go out for baseball?"

"Man, I'd love to, Dad," he agreed, "but I've got to keep my grade point up. You always said it was a balance: studies and sports and free time."

"Yeah, sometimes life is hard to balance with all the things you want to do, at one time, and you can't squeeze them all in. One thing I know: you're a hell of a ball player."

Shaun mimicked swinging a bat and made a clucking sound with his tongue in his mouth, as if a fastball had just been pounded out of a ballpark. I did a hushed impression of the roar of a crowd.

"Only thing is," Shaun went on, "I haven't played in a year. Only so much time."

He had no way of knowing it, but when he used that phrase, it brought my fears up again. But I forced a smile.

"I think we'd both agree," I suggested, "that fathers shouldn't pressure their sons to do things that they can't or don't want to do. But I'm going to just say it, straight up..."

"Uh-oh," he joked. "Here we go."

"One of my favorite moments ever was the day you hit that grand slam and won the game. Oh, and the league championship."

"I knew you were going to say that," Shaun stated.

"And I probably shouted so loud I embarrassed you," I offered. Shaun shifted his weight on the bench and moved in a little toward me, as if preparing a confession.

"No, I heard the ball hit the bat and ran the bases, and then I was rounding third, and that's when the crowd noise came to me. It was weird the way it was delayed like that. And of course, then, I saw you standing up, waving your arms around like mad. I couldn't hear you, with the crowd noise, but for sure, you were screaming and grabbing the chain link fence and shaking it."

We both sat there, happy in the memory.

"Hank Aaron's dad never yelled louder than I did," I bragged.

"You know the thing that impresses me the most about Hank?" Shaun asked. "Atlanta."

"Besides that."

"Twenty-five All-Star Games?"

"That too, but no."

I don't know why I said the next thing, but it just came out of my mouth. Maybe I was just hoping that Shaun would have a certain strength if I was taken away from him for any reason.

"I know you already know this," I murmured, "but it's just amazing how he never publicly complained when he got death threats and racist letters, and then went ahead and broke the Babe's record."

Shaun shook his head, sheepishly. "No, that's not what I was going to say. But it should have been."

"No, no, I'll shut up. Tell me." His head hung, probably thinking about the personal journey Aaron went through. "Shaun, I promise. I won't say a word. What were you thinking?"

Shaun looked up into my face. "You know the way a lot of players today are physically huge? You know, they've used performance-enhancing drugs, steroids, whatever, to give them an advantage? When I watch old videos of Hank, he didn't look ripped, totally muscular. I saw a guy whose eyes were sharper and whose wrists were faster than anyone on the field."

"Exactly," I grinned. "He had skills, man."

"He was born with them. And he built on them his whole life."

"'Course, he doesn't have the home run record anymore," Shaun conceded.

"He had it for quite a while," I countered. "And he won it the right way. And he's in the Hall of Fame."

I followed Shaun as we approached the end of our walk. Together, we walked back into the house and down the hallway toward his room. I could have spent hours there on the patio, talking to him about his future, about my childhood, about the challenges of getting through this world with as little damage to your reputation as possible. But he had homework, and it was my second visit of the day with him. There was no point annoying his mother after such a brief but uplifting visit.

Shaun walked a couple paces ahead of me, almost as tall as I was.

"Good luck out there in the Sunshine State," he offered over his shoulder.

"Thanks. I'll call you from the road, let you know how it's going."

He got to his bedroom door and as much as I didn't want to consider it, in a flash, I realized a phony charge could prevent me from hugging my son again. I instantly reached out, threw my arms around him and lifted him a few inches off the carpeting in a bear hug.

He grunted a little, turned and faced me. "You staying for some dessert or something?"

"I've got to talk with your mom privately, but I'll see you in a week or so."

He nodded and opened the door to his bedroom and left it open as he headed to his desk.

I very quietly closed it and found Emily sitting on the couch in the living room, a mostly empty glass of white wine in front of her. She was looking vacantly at an old black-and-white movie on TV, with no sound on.

"Want some wine?" she offered, and I saw that there was a clean glass set aside for me on the table alongside the edge of the sofa.

It had been a long time since Emily and I had had a conversation that wasn't about Shaun or money or what went wrong or what our responsibilities were as divorced parents. Just to be asked to have a couple sips of wine sounded so good, and yet I was suspicious about what might come out of any discussion in that moment. But I had promised to chat with her, and I wasn't about to take a chance on an early exit and possible resentment.

I sat on the sofa, a safe distance away. "No, but thanks. We had a great talk, about baseball and ethics. And time. We've brought up an amazing young man."

Emily swirled the remainder of her white wine, studying it but not drinking it. "Yeah, we did. Other things didn't work out, but Shaun is going to be all right."

It sounded like she sensed I was in some kind of trouble and was trying to figure out a way to get me to talk about it, which I was most definitely not going to do.

"What's going on with you and Cindy?" she asked, point blank.

"I think I might have mentioned, perhaps in passing, Emily, that we're now divorced.

Well, it's not official yet, but she filed for it."

"You said. But you didn't say much."

"It hurts. I'm talking about it all the time with my shrink. And of course, it's a little strange to talk about it with you, of all people."

"So that's it, then?" she protested. "I don't get to hear anything, whether you might get back together again or—"

"Emily, let's make a deal here. I'm really tired, and this is dangerous territory. Can we just have a couple questions on it and call it a night?"

"Sure. I mean, I wasn't clear if it was a fight or it was officially done or what."

"I told you. She wants a divorce and I'm not going to fight her on it. There's no going back. I don't want to go back. Okay?"

"Okay, okay. I'm sorry I asked."

I didn't mean to be a pain in the ass, but this divorce was so fresh. Couldn't she sense that I was hurting? She'd never been very good at that, though, the whole reading-a-room thing. Even though her lack of tact was frustrating, it was nice to sit on the couch with her, just to sit with someone who felt like family. I wondered if she'd visit me if I wound up in jail. She had no obligation to, but it'd be comforting to see her. I didn't want to think about that now though. I wanted to just soak in the moment. I stayed until she finished the last bit of wine in her glass, then I gave her a hug, holding her just a bit longer than I normally would. She seemed a little weirded out, but with the wine in her system, she didn't question my embrace.

It took me three minutes of driving home before I rounded a corner too sharply and brushed the concrete with one of my tires. The car shimmied slightly, and it brought me out of my head and back into my body.

I took a few deep breaths and could feel my blood pressure slow down. I didn't want to be home by myself in my hotel room, so I just cruised the streets I had grown up in, aimlessly, letting my mind wander. I lowered the windows in front and let the coolness of the early evening air brace me.

There was the house where I used to study with a friend. I turned a corner and there was another home that brought the memory of watching baseball with a friend on the weekend on TV, munching on the lunch their parents had made for us. I wound through the streets, moving away from the residential area, skirting the western edge, nearer to the highways. I suppose my thoughts had strayed again to the road trip I was about to take, to leaving my hometown and facing the uncertainty ahead.

So when I saw the two baseball fields shrouded in the dwindling night light, the diamonds where I had played and where Shaun showed his growing power, agility and confidence, I pulled up and parked right away. The chain-link gate was padlocked at that hour, of course, but I got a youthful burst of enthusiasm. Looking around guiltily to make sure no one was watching me, I climbed over a lower area of the fencing. Getting arrested for sitting alone in a closed ballpark seemed like the least of my worries. The field closest to me was not the one where Shaun had won the championship—that was off in the distance—but the two dugouts, basepaths and bleachers in front of me brought another warm memory.

I retraced my steps the best that I could to a time before. I wandered in the dark, trying to find the right spot where I had been, during the game, on the smooth, wooden benches. I eventually found it, and I sat to the left of home plate.

It was a Saturday afternoon Little League game I had come to in order to watch Shaun play. I sat and looked at home plate and the white lines running up to first and third. The game was tied 4-4, with a man on first, two out and the top of the ninth inning. It was always a pleasure to watch my son play, whether he did well or not, and whether his team won or not. But this game was particularly close and I was feeling the thrill and intensity of parents and friends in the stands, yelling their heads off, worried, excited, their knees bouncing up and down in anticipation of the next crack of the bat.

But the Saturday afternoon, 4-4 game took on a deeper meaning for me because it also marked the moment that I began looking for a new partner in my life. Both male and female friends and work associates had recommended dating apps, and the whole idea just seemed so strange and unnatural to me that I made little effort to try them out. But before I got in my car and drove to the ballpark that afternoon, I took out my cell phone and tried a dating site that a few people claimed they knew and liked. I skimmed through some profiles without contacting any of them, but I figured I might go back to the app if there were slow moments in the game.

After four innings, sure enough, there was no score. So I began flicking my way through some photos and profiles posted by women who lived in Cobb County. How can you pick a future mate based on a nice photo and five hundred words? It seemed absurd, but after more than six months, I felt socially cut off and unbalanced, so I decided to make the effort.

The opposing team finally scored a runner from second on a base hit in the bottom of the fifth, and the others sitting around me began lightly bouncing their knees in anticipation. I didn't. Showing my calmness and faith in my son's team, I began scrolling the dating site again. And that is the moment I saw Cindy. Her eyes had a sparkle that came through a small cell phone screen sitting outside in the Georgia sun. She had a huge smile on her face in every single picture she had posted. I found it refreshing after a slew of serious images. There were so many women trying to be models, but Cindy seemed natural, down to earth. And it's no surprise she smiled so often, with dimples punctuating both of her round cheeks and teeth that were a perfect shade of pearly white. She was an OB-GYN doctor, clearly successful and happy, and what she wrote about helping other women who were in need of health care and understanding moved me. She also had a few jokes in her profile which showed me she had a sense of humor, like "My ideal date is anything that doesn't involve the opera. I don't have the attention span for three hours of Italian vocals." That made me chuckle.

I took my time composing an introductory message from my profile, occasionally looking up to check out the progress of the game. I kept making sure I wasn't misspelling anything so I wouldn't look like an idiot. Finally, I went with, "Hi Cindy, I think you have the most beautiful smile I've ever seen. I'd love to meet up for coffee or a drink some time." When I finished typing it out, I didn't send it at first. Then, the opposing team was retired, leading 5-4, and I took it as a good omen that they didn't score anymore and clicked "send."

The game began to develop, and I didn't hear any promising or annoying "pings" or bells on my phone, so I tucked it into the back pocket of my jeans, rested my face in my hands and studied the ball game that had become all tied up in the top of the ninth inning with my son at bat.

Just as Shaun had talked about on the patio, I knew he couldn't hear me shouting his name when he was up. It was his job to focus on the pitcher, on his own breathing, rhythm, his muscular memory when he knew it was right to make that split second decision to whip the bat into position. You can't be listening for what your dad is yelling to you forty feet away in a moment like that. But there I was, along with all the other supporters of his team, raising our voices, hooting and shrieking like birds, pounding on the benches, hoping to see the moment that would change the game in our favor.

At the exact moment that Shaun lashed out and caught the ball on the fat part of the barrel, just before our part of the stands exploded in noisy reaction, I heard the "ping" of the phone. I was stunned but couldn't deal with it because, in unison, I rose with the other people on our side of the stands and watched the majestic, towering fly Shaun had driven to left center.

But when all the activity was over, I remembered my phone had pinged. And I was glad I remembered because it was a reply message from Cindy. It read, "Hello, handsome." My heart was beating even faster than when I'd seen the home run. But then, her first message disappeared from the screen. A second came up. But it vanished not more than two seconds after she sent it. And it made no sense at the time, but I remembered only one word in the second instant message from Cindy.

It was the word, "Stop."

NOT MARRIAGE MATERIAL

There was something agonizingly sweet about sitting in my car, outside my grey and white family home, waiting to say goodbye to my mother and talking on my cell with Sabrina. Although he didn't realize it, I had just said my final goodbye to Shaun the night before. Now, I just had a few more errands before heading off to Florida.

"Are you nervous about talking with Mom?" Sabrina asked on the other end of the phone line.

"A little. But she believes in me and thinks I'm doing the right thing, so that's a huge help."

"And how are the other people in your life treating you?" she teased me gently.

"No reply from Cindy, of course. Emily wants more info and I can't give it to her. Shaun is great, though I hated to lie to him. Listen, if I have to, are you all right with relaying information to Mom while I'm down there?"

"Of course," she immediately agreed. "We have Sunday dinners, so I can keep her posted."

"Thanks so much." The white, floral front curtains parted, and I saw my mother wave to me and motion me to come on in. I held up a finger in the air, indicating it would be one more minute.

"I'm going in now, to talk to her," I told Sabrina. "I don't think anyone is going to find me at Ron's, but in case they do, I want you and her to hear it directly from me, not from the papers or some cop or court."

"You'll be all right down there," she said, and the strength in her tone helped me believe it.

"Thanks, sis."

"Call me from the road," she said, and I promised I would.

Mothers always want to feed their children, even when they're adults. It doesn't matter how old you are, how plump you are or if you're even hungry. Their many ways of expressing love includes the comfort and sustenance of food. And that's why when I visited my mother, we usually convened in the kitchen. Even if it wasn't a full meal, she always had snacks like molasses cookies or crumb cake or something she had whipped up to put a smile on my face.

But this time was more serious, so instead of assembling a plate of finger food, I gently guided her, one arm around her shoulders, into her living room. I sat her down on the sofa and went to the curtains that she kept closed, now struggling with the fear of her son being arrested. I yanked them open with an exaggerated flair and looked back at her with a wide smile. The mid-morning light flooded the room.

"It's a beautiful day. Let's have some light in here," I said.

"Sounds like something I used to say when you were little," she observed.

"Yeah, it does."

I sat down on the sofa next to her and just held her hand for the longest time. We both looked out into the little garden in front of the lawn, resting our eyes and our concerns for a while. Finally, reluctantly, she broke the silence.

"You think Cindy will be in touch?"

"No, Mama. I think the only way I'm ever going to hear from her again is through a divorce attorney. And you know what? That's fine. If she or her attorney contact you—"

"Tell them to take a hike!"

That got a smile out of me. "Or words to that effect, if you like."

"Emily?"

"Say nothing."

"My baby Shaun?"

That one stopped me in my tracks, but not for long. "Just make him feel loved. But no, I have to keep him out of this. I've got it set up this way. The only people who are going to call you with any news at all are either me or Sabrina."

My mother squeezed my hand and looked me so deep in the eyes that I felt myself sink a little into the thick cushions.

"You sure are lucky to have a sister who looks out for you."

My mother's eyes were not tear-filled, but they were slightly glossy. I didn't want either of us to cry in this moment, and I tried my hardest to hold myself together.

"I'm so sorry you're doing this alone," she said.

"I'm not alone, Mama. You and Sabrina are looking out for me." I clutched her hand and kissed her cheek.

"I know, but I just wish Emily or Cindy had stuck by your side." She shook her head gently.

I nodded. "Me too, but life doesn't always work out like we want."

She quickly removed her glasses, wiped away some moisture, put the glasses back on, and rested her head on my shoulder. I wished we could freeze that moment.

~

The next day, I had an appointment with Dr. Warren. Unlike my mother, he grimaced more than he smiled. It was unsettling at first, talking to a grimacing stranger about my deepest issues, but I'd started to accept that it was just his way. And I had to admit, I looked forward to my sessions, especially this one. I had a lot to say, and it felt good to get it all off my chest. At some point during my ramble, Dr. Warren held up his hand, as if to pause or course-correct.

"I'm here to help, Tyler, and I'm glad to do it, but I want to interject because you just mentioned a lot of important things. There's room to go deeper on some of these topics. For instance—"

"Oh! I'm sorry. I know things were tense the last time we talked, and I do want you to know how much I appreciate your guiding me through this mess."

Dr. Warren smiled as he jotted something down on his clipboard. "As I say, it's my responsibility to help you. And it seems like you need some clarity on the situation with Cindy in order to heal. So let's see if we can figure this out. Let me ask you, Tyler, what was the first thing Cindy revealed to you that suggested she might be unfaithful?"

"Oh, she didn't *suggest* she might be unfaithful. She came out and admitted it. In the beginning, spending the nights with each other, Cindy told me things that kind of shocked me. There was an affair she had with a married man that ended her first marriage. I mean, our sexual connection at that point was pretty strong. I didn't need wild stories to stay interested in Cindy physically. But I think she really enjoyed seeing how surprised I looked when she got going with her sex stories."

"Sex stories," he repeated, allowing the phrase to sit there in the office air for me to think about. "That's significant…and do we know if she was telling the truth about her affair and the end of her first marriage?"

"What can I say? She literally told me it was an incredible turn-on being with someone else's husband. I thought, 'This is wild, but what if she gets tired of me?'"

"Yes, that would potentially be a problem. Assuming, however, Tyler, that this wasn't some kind of erotic game that a new couple might experiment in."

I shook my head from side to side, giving him a look of disappointment. "After time passed, and we grew closer, Cindy would go on these crying jags. She would be filled with doubt about being an OB-GYN. She would say to me, 'I feel like I'm going crazy.' No reason at all. I'd ask. All she'd give me is some vague reason for her to question being a doctor. And she was respected. So what was that about?"

Dr. Warren decided to merely note down the quote, rather than to take a guess.

"And any ideas I had about her creating imaginary sex scenarios for fun ended when Cindy swore to me, very upset, that she had had an affair with a married pastor at a church she went to before we met."

"Which church?" Dr. Warren immediately asked.

"I don't know. I guess a church she used to go to. But that's nothing in comparison to the day that she was crying hysterically and told me that she had gotten a death threat phone call from a guy who she had broken it off with suddenly. Again, some guy she was with before me. Now, do those stories sound like fun erotic ideas for a new couple, Doctor?"

"No, they don't. But you must admit, they also sound like someone who was sexually adventuresome."

"Sexually adventuresome?" I asked, although I knew what he meant. I repeated the question, half to Dr. Warren and half to myself. She *was* sexually adventuresome...but I still didn't totally get why that was relevant. I saw flashes of Cindy in those early years, images of her face popping into my consciousness and then disappearing like a slideshow. That's when Dr. Warren broke me out of my thought pattern with a new question.

"So maybe Cindy, who was sexually adventuresome, was in love with you and trying to settle down, to find a way to be with you that was very different from her past. That probably put a lot of pressure on you." He looked at me then, gauging my reaction. It *did* put a lot of pressure on me. I nodded before he continued. "It also indicates something about the possible motivation behind her reactions. When you suspected her of being unfaithful, she may have been experiencing immense pressure too. You get what I mean, Tyler?"

"I'm not sure I do," I admitted.

Dr. Warren removed his glasses. "I'm saying that some of us are just built differently. We've acknowledged Cindy as sexually adventuresome. That's who she was when you met her, and when you fell in love with her. And it sounds like she wanted to be the 'good wife' with you. Maybe she wanted to be loyal, but at the same time, she found it difficult. It was against her nature."

"But...does that make her actions defensible?"

"I'm not trying to defend her, Tyler. I think what she did to you is awful. But it's helpful to explore these things from every angle. Clarity is the goal today, remember?"

"She told me what she had done. I didn't like it, but I didn't leave her. What did I get? I got more revelations, more breakdowns, and then more secrecy. She was setting herself up to ruin our relationship."

"I hear what you're saying, Tyler. Maybe Cindy felt if she was totally honest, you would accept all that, not doubt her, not stalk her into her office and—"

"Stop right there." I was getting annoyed. "I told you before, I had every right to suspect her, and I did not stalk her."

"I agree! I agree. Okay, I'm sorry. I got ahead of myself. I was just suggesting that she might have seen it another way. In fact, you're dealing with chronic pain from falling down the stairs, and anyone would understand if this confused your memory about what happened between you and Cindy. It's completely understandable."

I furrowed my eyebrows and scratched the corner of my ear. I could feel Dr. Warren's gaze on me, probably waiting for a response, psychoanalyzing my facial expressions. I didn't feel like talking anymore, but then he broke the silence again.

"Did I say something that upset you?"

"Umm…" I thought about it for a moment.

"It's okay. You can tell me if I said something upsetting. That's how this works."

"I just…I guess I feel like the victim here. I don't feel like I did anything wrong."

"I'm not trying to say you did anything wrong. It's my job to help you see your issues through different angles. Part of that is exploring Cindy's perspective on all this."

"But it's not like I trapped her. She wanted to marry me. She wanted to settle down together. We agreed we wanted to be exclusive, hence why we got married."

"Right, and I understand that, Tyler, I do. I'm just saying that while, yes, it seems that you did nothing wrong in this scenario, you also selected a woman who was perhaps…what's the word…" He looked up as if to search for the word on the ceiling. "Not marriage material! That's what I'm trying to say. Perhaps your only mistake was picking someone who was unavailable."

"Oh…I see. I haven't thought about it like that before."

"That's why I'm here," he said, smirking.

I thanked him for his time and made my way out of his office, walking to my car a bit lighter with newfound clarity. I turned on the radio for the first time in weeks, letting the sounds of cool jazz take over, instead of the usual cacophony of thoughts.

FLASHBACKS AND FIDELITY

It was going to be a nine hour drive from Marietta to West Palm Beach, and I did not want to arrive too late to take Ron out to the nice dinner I had promised him on the phone. So, in the morning, I quickly packed a bag with clothes and my laptop, eating a breakfast of a travel cup of coffee and a microwaved egg-like concoction between two pieces of starchy substance. It was fine. It was hot, and I wanted to get out on the road early and beat the commuter traffic out of Cobb County.

I had a second bag, a smaller one, with things I needed in the front seat, like some snacks, my sunglasses and my filing cards, in case some memories suddenly came back to me. And, sadly, necessarily, I had my vials of pills with me in that case on the passenger's seat next to me.

The morning air on the highway refreshed me a bit, and I breathed it in rather than using the air conditioning of my car. In fact, the drive was so nice that I lost track of time for once. I had been driving about an hour and rather than worrying about jail or my family, I just experienced the flow of the air, the rush of passing and being passed by cars and trucks, the plain sensation of going. People think satisfaction only comes in terms of accomplishing goals, of being able to say to yourself, "I attained this," or "I fought for and won that." But while I headed due south on Interstate 75, just the thought of not surrendering had given me some hope. The fact that I didn't let that manipulative attorney in Cobb County talk me into turning myself in for some undisclosed charge meant that I was destined to fight, no matter the end result. It also meant that I had to find someone else to help me with my case, and I didn't know who that would be. I hoped Ron could help. It was upsetting to think that no one in my own county seemed prepared to help me.

But it was not the time to worry about that. I needed to find the right advocate who not only was knowledgeable about the law but willing to fight for me. Perhaps that was someone who didn't have any connections to Cobb County. And of course, that would reduce the lawyer's effectiveness. Still, I had to think in new ways to begin to resolve the puzzle I was in.

I pushed on, wanting to stick to the driving schedule and not arrive late and disappoint my host. I couldn't have been on the road for much more than an hour, and yet, it had been the most carefree I had been in so long. But as I got back onto the Interstate and sped up, my brain went somewhere that I didn't want it to go. I went back to the first trip Cindy and I took together after we began dating. We had decided it would be romantic to drive to Arizona and visit the Native American spiritual power spots, among the wonderful rock formations in Sedona.

As beautiful as that location is, my personal memory of going there with Cindy had great sorrow attached to it. On our last night vacationing in Sedona, Cindy broke down out of nowhere. One minute, we were enjoying a nice walk, observing the cacti, and the next, she was crying. She tried to hold it in, but eventually, the onslaught of tears made it so that she couldn't wear her sunglasses.

I remember asking her to look at me. I suggested we pause our walk so we could talk about it. She hung her head in embarrassment and admitted she was uncertain about her career pursuits. That was the first time she mentioned it.

"But you're great at everything you do," I told her.

She just shrugged and said, "Thank you. I think we should keep walking."

The memory set off a new round of pounding in my skull. It quickly became relentless, and I had to pull off onto the shoulder of the highway, take a pill and down it with coffee that was no longer warm. I put on my sunglasses and squinted, hoping the pain would subside soon. I had been truthful with Dr. Warren when I told him in his office that Cindy had crying bouts and serious doubts about being a doctor in service to other women, even though she refused to explain to me why she felt so unworthy of her profession.

What I didn't get around to admitting to Warren was that I began to feel I couldn't help her, and she desperately needed a lifeline. I knew she had a strong faith, and while I didn't go to her church, one day, holding her and wiping away the tears from her cheeks, I simply looked into her eyes and urged her, "Listen, you're a spiritual person. Why not rely on someone who you trust who gets who you are and can reach you, your heart, in a spiritual way? Wouldn't that make sense, rather than just beating yourself up?"

She saw I cared, and she saw I was worried, and to my great relief, Cindy agreed to find someone within her church who could counsel her. That led to her feeling a bit better and our discussion about going away together, somewhere in nature, where we could reconnect and put those early moments of misery behind us. And so, we decided on Sedona.

As the foliage along the Interstate whooshed by, my headache began to lessen a bit. I was now seeing Cindy and me, hand in hand, in shorts and t-shirts and backpacks, meandering through the surreal, beautiful rock formations in the Arizona sun. We took our time, sometimes just resting our hands on the wind-carved stones, trying to imagine what life was like for the people who lived there before it was ever settled. It was nice to be flooded by a pleasant memory for once. But that was no longer reality. I blinked my eyes and rubbed them with my fist, deciding I needed to focus on the present moment for once.

Even though I had punched in Ron's address and it came up on the GPS of my car, he lived in a West Palm development that had white townhouses with pastel-colored flourishes, and they all looked very similar. I wandered around a bit, trying to find the correct house number. Finally, I heard a door open behind me and a deep voice call out, "Hey, you some kind of salesman or something?"

I whirled, as best as I could, with my bags. There, in a doorway, stood Ron. He had a little less hair on his forehead and a little more waistline, but his disarming smile and outstretched arms reminded me how glad I was that we had met all those years ago in college and stayed friends. On the subject of "old school," Ron chose the Flagler Steakhouse, down a palm-lined road. We sat out on a terrace, relaxing quietly with drinks and admiring the view of the golf course.

"God, it's good to see you again," I blurted out.

"You too, brother," he agreed. "Thanks for agreeing to take me to my favorite place in town. The filet mignon here is amazing, but it ain't cheap."

"I'm sure we're going to love it." I started to yawn a little and raised the margarita glass to my mouth to try and disguise it.

"Long drive?" Ron guessed.

"Well, yeah. That, and the pills I have to take."

Ron looked concerned. "From one old college roommate to another, can we talk straight here, Ty? I mean, we hold nothing back?"

"That's exactly what I want and exactly what I need."

Ron swirled a piece of bread in some crab dip, munched on it and then decided to open up a bit. "I know you're going through a lot of stuff. The divorce. This legal stuff with Cobb County. But I've got to say. You look wiped out. And I don't mean just driving nine hours from Marietta."

"Well, it's like I say. The medicine takes it out of you."

Ron cleared his throat. "Medicine? Or pills? Ty, we both partied a bit when we were young, but I don't remember you being particularly into drugs of any kind back then. Is this pressure getting to you?"

At first, I didn't understand. Then, it dawned on me that Ron, who had not seen me in years, was now seeing me at my worst. Did I look like an addict?

"What? No, the psychiatrist. I got all kinds of pills for pain, for headaches, for memory problems, like I said."

"For memory problems," Ron repeated. "Yeah."

"What is that, a joke?"

Now, I truly was lost. "You think I'm kidding about memory loss, Ron? This is serious business. I have gaps in what I remember."

Ron's face grew long, and his voice softened. He reached across the table and place a big, bracing hand on my left shoulder and left it there. "I don't doubt it's a problem, and I don't doubt that it's serious, Ty. You know why? You never even told me about it."

I stared at him. He didn't move an inch, not a twitch of the eyelid, not the corner of his mouth. My voice caught a little in my throat. "Oh, man. I didn't tell you about the pills? Or the memory loss? When we talked on the phone?"

Ron simply, very slowly and sadly, shook his head from side to side.

"I'll tell you more about it during the weekend," I started cautiously, "but basically, I slipped on top of the stairs when I was with Cindy. The pain started there, and things started to go downhill for us from there."

I started to apologize for never telling him, but Ron wouldn't let me.

"You have enough to worry about. Hurting my feelings because you forgot something isn't going to be one of them."

And with perfect timing, our waitress came, carrying two plates sizzling and crackling with our steaks. She carefully set them down, arranged side platters of vegetables and condiments and asked us if there was anything else we needed.

"No, thanks," we said in unison.

Ron and I breathed in the delicious steam that came off the filets.

"Please tell me," Ron teased, "that short-term memory loss doesn't affect your appetite."

"No way." I smiled, and we both grabbed our knives and forks and hungrily began to eat.

Back at Ron's townhouse, I was full, sleepy and wearing a t-shirt and sweatpants. Ron was still wearing his work clothes, but he was contentedly patting his stomach and had clearly enjoyed the dinner. I showed him some photos of Shaun on my cell phone, as well as the less- than-spectacular home where I was temporarily living.

"The place is just a rental. I don't know why I even took pictures of it," I mumbled. Ron wrapped me up in a bearhug, which I returned with gratitude.

"Don't worry. We'll figure all this out. Dinner was so good."

"I love that place," I agreed.

"Help yourself to anything you want in the kitchen, if you get up before me," Ron offered, and we said goodnight to each other.

I let out a groan of tired contentment as I crawled into the guest bed. I was tired, ready to sleep, but something nagged at the back of my mind. Instead of turning off my cell phone, I continued to scroll back through the history of my photos.

Did I still have any of Cindy left? I couldn't remember. That wasn't a cruel joke. I did not recall whether I ever decided to just erase her image from my photo collection, or if I needed some reminder of her, when she was at her best, when we were truly happy, no matter how fleeting.

As it turned out, I had grouped some photos of Cindy into a folder, showing her at various times during our marriage. Strangely enough, one of the shots was at the cottage in the foothills of Sedona. It was Cindy, wrapped demurely in one of the golden, fluffy towels, after we had made love and I had secretly decided that we would be married. Her expression was blissful, content and even a little shy, which was so unlike her.

Another memory came back, one that I had completely lost. It wasn't about the beauty of the moment. It had come later, before we left the cottage and began driving back to Georgia. I scrambled out of bed and wildly tore through the smaller bag I had brought. With my hands suddenly shaking, I clawed through until I found a pen and the stack of notecards. I brought them back to the bed, sat up against the backboard and pulled out a new three-by-five card and began to print carefully on it.

"CINDY ON BED, SEDONA, BEFORE WE LEAVE. SHE CRIES, SAYS I CAN DO BETTER THAN MARRYING HER."

I hadn't actually proposed. I was going to think of something wonderfully romantic and splashy, like in a romantic comedy film, once we got back to Marietta. But somehow, perhaps by my facial expression, she must have known what I was thinking, planning. With utter despair, Cindy threw herself across the bed in our room, her lungs heaving, her tears unstoppable.

There was no comforting her, once again. "Cindy, honey. This has been a magical trip. We're celebrating being together. There's no reason to cry."

She hid her face in the blanket, but I could make out her muffled voice. "No, no, no," she sobbed. "It can't work. Not with me. It will never work."

"Yes, it will," I insisted, and I gently pulled her curly, damp hair away from her face so she could breathe easier. "I promise you, it will work. Until death do we part."

It was clearly a mistake to find the photos of Cindy again. Even bringing back a forgotten memory, a painful one, didn't seem like it would be of any use to me. And once again, the pain reared behind my eyes. I popped up and grabbed another pain pill, but instead of taking it, I thought about Ron's disturbed reaction when I had mentioned the pills for the first time at Flagler's. It had nearly ruined our wonderful dinner together.

I didn't want to go without sleep. I didn't want to struggle for hours in pain, trying to use a warm washcloth instead of medicine that would do a better job, but it felt like more memories were coming back to me on their own, and that the pills might be a way of blocking them.

So I went to Ron's guest bathroom and ran hot water over a small washcloth. I got it steaming, squeezed out the excess water, turned off the tap and the lights and got back into bed. I turned off my phone and plugged it into the charger that lay on the nearby nightstand. Then, I clicked off the small lamp, pressed the hot washcloth deep down into my eye sockets and lay on top of the covers, trying to relax and keep my mind off of the ache I felt.

That pain was not going away. I decided I would distract it, guide it. I knew that Cindy was going to be part of my guided memory, but it didn't necessarily mean I had to think of a bad association to her. And then I knew what to do. I would relive the excitement of when Shaun hit the home run just as Cindy contacted me on the dating app. That was a wonderful memory, but how could I remember exactly the sweet things that she had said?

There was a way. I had never deleted the app from my cell phone. So, once again, taking the now cooled washcloth from my eyes, I sat up, turned on the lamp and my phone, opened the app and found the earliest message from Cindy. I was amazed to see that my memory was absolutely correct.

Her first message to me, on that Saturday at the baseball field, was exactly as I had recalled it.

"HELLO, HANDSOME."

But next came the second message from her, one that appeared so fast while Shaun trotted triumphantly around the bases that it had never fully registered in my mind. But now, I was staring at it on my cell phone screen, and it horrified me.

Cindy had typed, "I'm warning you to keep the hell away from me!"

It was pretty ironic, considering what she and I had been through, but obviously, after saying hello to me for the first time, that message was not meant for me. And if it was meant for another man, and I had paid more attention, would I have even become involved with Cindy? It was a good question to ask. But what I had also forgotten about, since the accident on the stairs, was the third message, the apology, that Cindy had sent right after her accidental message.

"Sorry, Tyler. That was a message to a man who keeps asking me out even though I tell him to leave me alone. I would like to go out with you, though. Very much."

SEXUALLY TRANSMITTED EVIDENCE

I must have rolled around uncomfortably during the night because I awoke both groggy and with a stiff neck. I wandered downstairs hoping to share a cup of coffee with Ron, but he was long gone. He'd left a note on the kitchen table, advising, "Get some extra rest today. You deserve it."

I felt fortunate that I had a little time away from the chaos of Marietta. Debating whether to eat first or do so after a shower and a change of clothes, my rumbling stomach won out. I explored the kitchen. Unlike my rented, temporary home and its frozen and unhealthy eating choices, Ron had fresh foods. In a cabinet over the sink, I found a cardboard container of steel-cut oats that I decided would be a good way to begin the day, rather than going out for some drive-through fast food in the general vicinity.

After carefully boiling a saucepan of oats, I meandered through his refrigerator and was pleased to find both blueberries and dark raspberries. I sprinkled a few on top of a now heaping bowl of oatmeal, drizzled some low-fat milk on top and slowly enjoyed it as I reviewed the three-by-five cards I had laid out on his kitchen table.

I shuffled back and forth through my timeline, staring briefly at each card, hoping for some blazing realization that would suddenly excite and motivate me to action. While the quiet twittering of birds outside brought me a little relaxation, I got no new insights. There were no clues as to where to begin, where to jump in.

While it was again painful to relive the past, it did seem to make sense to work back to Cindy and me on our Sedona trip. It was still fresh in my mind since I had thought about it a good deal. But I remembered that Cindy was pretty secretive about her private life at that point in our marriage. The secrets in the beginning were for erotic purposes and then, when that faded, I no longer seemed to have a right to be curious about anything she did.

And if Dr. Warren was correct about Cindy's psychology, then there was a kind of mental collapse she went through when I confronted her at the hospital. I saw her anger and denial and refusal to even talk to me as an unspoken admission of guilt. I decided then and there that it was infidelity. I believed I was right and couldn't imagine another explanation. But if that wasn't the case, if it was a male or female friend who, sad to say, Cindy felt she could confide in more than me, what would that feel like to her?

I finished putting the dishes in the dishwasher, dried my hands on a towel and sat down again at the breakfast table. To abruptly change the locks of our house suggested Cindy had decided then and there that she didn't want to be with me anymore. She must have cleared her schedule to spend hours to find a divorce attorney who would drop everything and file a writ. By the end of my work day, I got served with papers, couldn't enter our former home and couldn't even get Cindy on the phone to work something out. It had to be Cindy in a state of panic, or fury, or perhaps both. And if I was wrong about it being her cheating on me, then what else was it?

I resumed looking through the cards I had written just before we left Sedona and stopped again on the one that described Cindy lying across the bed in the golden robe, unbearably sad, crying, insisting that she would never be worthy of being with me. Was that it? Cindy, at the hospital, being hit full in the face with the realization that her behavior, even if she wasn't being unfaithful, would never measure up as my wife? But rather than admitting her own weakness, maybe she simply counterattacked, trying to get as much out of the sudden death of our marriage as possible.

In a way, it didn't make sense, because Cindy was filled with self-loathing and guilt. I expected her to come back from the hospital after the confrontation, sit down quietly and either admit to an affair or say she felt like she was not psychologically balanced enough to be my wife, or anyone else's for that matter. But that last gasp of vulnerability I expected from Cindy never happened. Her rage and then complete retreat became one of the most disturbing and incomprehensible moments of my entire life.

I decided to go upstairs, take a shower and see if a soothing stream of warm water could help me make sense of it all. I remember how the water from the showerhead soothed us both. We comfortably, lovingly soaped each other's bodies, rinsed each other off and then headed for the plush comfort of our oversized towels. Why was I thinking of that isolated time in the shower with Cindy, in the distant past, while alone in Ron's guest bedroom? I squeezed my eyes tight, trying to pick up any mental details that would make it significant. The memory faded under the steam, and it seemed that it wasn't isolated at all, just a random and strangely sweet and familiar bathing ritual.

I wrapped a big, purple bath towel Ron had laid out for me around my shoulders and sawed back and forth, gently absorbing the moisture. I gave up the idea of any notecard memories for the moment and went to the drawer Ron provided me to get some underwear. And that is when I remembered. I didn't see her face at first. I did remember she was idly drying the rest of my back.

The flashback was triggered by her tone of surprise, maybe even of alarm. I remember when she stopped rubbing my shoulders. "What is *that?*" she asked. Looking at the spot on my right calf now, in the present moment, assured me that I wasn't creating an imaginary conversation. It was barely visible, but the scar was there, and I was stock still, concentrating, waiting for the buried dialogue.

"What?" I asked her. "This bump? I know. It's been there a few weeks. I thought it was a wart or something, but it hasn't gone away."

In my mind, Cindy shifted her weight and focus, and both of us, still covered in our towels, were face to face. I was puzzled, but she was haunted.

"That's not a wart," Cindy said, her voice strained.

"What is it, then?" I asked, but by her tone, I didn't want to know. Her eyes were downcast as she summoned the courage to look up again, meet my expression head-on and hope for my understanding.

"When I was nineteen," Cindy began, "I had a boyfriend, and while we were very attracted to each other, and very passionate about each other..." Her voice trailed off.

I sensed where the story was going, and I was angry because of her hesitation. "Finish it!"

She jumped a little and nodded. "Herpes. He gave me herpes."

"And now you've given it to me," I said coldly.

"I'm sorry, Tyler. I was just a stupid kid. I was nineteen and I didn't know any—"

"You're a *doctor*, Cindy. How can you be an MD and not be honest about this?"

I must have risen angrily from the bed, wanting to get away from her, wrapped in my towel, betrayed. Of course, the conversation faded, but I had seen her shame and her inability to answer. Not quite dry after my shower but not willing to forget any details, I dashed for my notecards. I found my hands shaking with anger. I breathed deeply, let it out and in block letters wrote:

"CINDY ADMITS GETTING HERPES AT 19."

I rushed to get dressed, even though I wasn't even clear what I could do with this new information. I had my shoes on when a disturbing thought intruded: If Cindy waited years before admitting to me that she had herpes, how many other men had she infected? And, even worse, were there men that she had warned, giving them more respect than she'd done for me?

My brain was jumbled now with thoughts, and I felt queasy, light-headed. I wanted to take some medication but again sensed it was better to be open to the insights that were coming my way. I needed to go somewhere, to get a little distance from Ron's, just for a while, before telling him over dinner what I had recalled about Cindy's dishonesty. I was ready to go downstairs and lock the door with the key Ron gave me, but I stopped upstairs, looked around. I still felt dizzy, disoriented. I had my personal bag and wasn't forgetting anything, or so I thought.

My eyes set upon a small area rug near the stairs. It was strange that I hadn't noticed it before. Of course, my mind bent back in time to my tripping on the rug that Cindy and I had in our house. I still couldn't be sure whether that rug Cindy and I had owned, tacked down, was eventually moved to the very edge of the staircase—a purposely loose, dangerous position. I had taken that slow-motion tumble, head-over-heels, jarring my mind, many times. I didn't know what to believe yet, but I felt a surge of energy.

Leaping into my car as I switched my brain's channel back to reality, I made a mental note to find a health clinic. I needed to get tested for herpes again, and any other sexually transmitted diseases I could think of along the way. In my GPS, I plugged in the restaurant where I'd be meeting Ron for dinner. I found a pleasant, upscale place, not too busy for us. The hostess greeted us with a timid smile as she led us to our booth, our menus folded between her arms.

"I think I'll go easy on you tonight," he said cheerfully, once we got settled at our table. "No need, my man," I said, an enigmatic smile crossing my lips. "In fact, I kind of had some breakthroughs in memory today. So, I insist that we both celebrate tonight."

Ron's eyes glimmered with interest. "Really? What did you remember?" I was going to have fun with a rush of revelations, but I decided to hold off for the time being.

The waitress came and we ordered drinks, appetizers, entrees and when we clinked glasses, Ron said tartly, "My job's not that interesting or hard. So, let's go, Ty. I want to hear some dirt."

He saw me react a little and withdrew the word. "Sorry. Some news."

I leaned in, looking around, and then agreed. "It is kind of outrageous, Ron, but I know that it's true. I remembered it clearly, and it changes *everything*."

I took out the block-printed notecard about Cindy admitting to me she had herpes when she was nineteen. Rather than revolted, Ron seemed fascinated, which was good, because I was in a storytelling role, and I also didn't want to put him off his dinner.

There was an eventual pause in my memories about Cindy, and he gently filled in a comment.

"Not only did she keep it a secret as a doctor," Ron observed, "but you don't know how many other guys she spread it to."

"You're right," I agreed. "I'll never know."

"I'm not telling you what to do, but I would get tested again. For everything."

"Way ahead of you, brother. I'm going to a local clinic first thing in the morning."

"Wow." Ron pushed back his plate, pondered the new information he'd been given and gave a low whistle. "I'm just glad this stuff is coming back to you. We're going to figure out what's going on, and I want to help you do it with a minimum of those pills."

"And! Cindy breaking her vow as a doctor also means that it calls into question all the other games that were going on," I emphasized.

Ron's eyes got really wide. "Like seeing a guy on the side and not telling you?'

"Maybe. Maybe not, Ron." Ron didn't get it at first. "Well, what's more of a betrayal than cheating on your husband, huh?"

Ron's eyes got real wide as he stated, "She could be removed from her medical practice." I was glad Ron was on the same wavelength as me. Silence hung over the table, both of us deep in our private thoughts.

"That wouldn't bode well with a jury."

"My thoughts exactly." I smirked as I took a sip from my drink, the condensation coating my hand in moisture.

"Man," Ron suddenly exclaimed, "I am never getting married again!"

I let out a much-needed roar of laughter. This drew the attention of our waitress, and Ron and I engaged in the age-old competition of offering to pay the bill. I grabbed his card and flipped it back to him.

"Bring this gentleman the dessert cart. I can't thank him enough for hosting me."

The waitress took my card and made a smiling, subtle escape. Ron put his credit card back into his wallet, but when he looked up again, he looked at me with curiosity. I was writing furiously on another notecard: "CINDY CHECKS MADE OUT TO 'CASH.'"

"You are on fire," Ron said, beaming. "But, uh, what does it mean?"

"I found some checks she had written, large ones from her business account, for 'Cash.' I called and asked why, thinking it was for a guy she was having an affair with. She got mad, told me it was none of my business. The next day, I'm served with divorce papers, she's accusing me of stalking her at work, and the locks have been changed on the house."

"How could she do all that so fast?" Ron asked. "I've never

processed anything that quickly. There just isn't a way to draft and serve papers in a day. Someone had to be helping her."

HELPFUL FRIENDS

There was the sensation of discovery, of multiple realizations that came from me when Ron and I had our second dinner together. It was true that I felt a breakthrough, even though I was still stumbling in the dark. That was why I delayed my revelations to Ron and even surprised myself with the recalled memory of finding Cindy making checks out for cash to someone and not revealing to me who it was. I had insisted Ron survey the desserts and despite his patting his belly in protest, he looked the choices over, selected a piece of German chocolate cake and we waited. I had told him I was full, and although it was true, he looked a little disappointed.

We had left the Cindy question open on the table, how it appeared that she'd had some kind of legal help to so rapidly reverse gears on me.

"I'm done," Ron said after a few bites of the cake I made him order. He clattered the fork onto his plate, not really in satisfaction but more in submission. "But it's really good," he protested and slid the plate my way. I dug out a piece of the gooey cake from the side he hadn't tried and savored it. "You finish it," he offered.

"I'm on a diet," I lied. I had another big dollop of chocolate and coconut icing, and we headed home, not exactly disappointed about the discussion we'd had but also aware that it had raised even more questions. The food and lateness of the hour had made us groggy and mostly silent on the way back to his condo.

"I'm going to get up this time and have breakfast with you," I promised, as we prepared to turn in for the night.

"Don't make promises you can't keep," he joked and then softened his tone. "It's great having you around, man. You know you can stay as long as you like."

"I know," I said. "Thank you. Let's see how things go tomorrow. I'm caught between wanting to kick down the doors of justice—"

"Yeah?"

"—and hanging out with you in every watering hole in West Palm and wishing it would all go away."

"Give that brain a rest," Ron advised, "and I'll see you at breakfast."

I went to the guest bedroom and changed into some comfortable sleepwear. I washed up, brushed my teeth and then felt the familiar pain, the slight pounding in my head. Would it progress into a monstrous headache that would keep me up? I reminded myself that by avoiding my meds, I had really done some important exploration. Did I really want to risk undoing the memory recall that could change things for the better?

I stared into my open palm in the bathroom, studying the tablet, contemplating taking half of it and hopefully getting a good night's sleep. Before I could pour a glass of water, however, my cell phone buzzed. I felt myself stiffen. Of course, I didn't have to take any calls I didn't want to take, but it was the idea that the DA's office or the sheriff or even the Georgia Bureau of Investigation was tracking me, closing in.

With some fear as to who would appear on my Caller ID, I went over to the plugged-in phone. A smile crossed my face. I took the phone out of the charger, flopped onto the bed comfortably and sighed happily into the phone.

"The one person I want to talk to," I admitted. "I've had a real whirlwind of a day. I'm sorry I didn't call earlier. Are you okay?"

"Sure," Sabrina said, radiating confidence. "Everything is normal." She gave a small chuckle, and we shared a laugh. "Well, as a normal as things go 'round here."

I wondered what to say next. She waited, but not for long. "It sounds like you found out some things. Tell me all about it."

I wanted to tell her about the memory of Cindy admitting she had herpes, but I wasn't sure my sister would want those kinds of details. And besides, I wanted to get the lab results from the clinic, in case I had to prepare myself for better medical news. I said a silent prayer that I'd be all right and tried to briefly explain.

"It's pretty important, and if I can verify it, Cindy has broken the law and I'll have a claim against her. I'm waiting on some confirmation, and then I want to tell you in person."

"Okay," Sabrina agreed, stretching out the syllables, sounding unsure. "Was there something else, Tyler?"

She was too smart for me. But I didn't feel comfortable discussing the rumor Ron and I had batted around about Cindy writing out checks behind my back, possibly to frame me.

"I'm sorry, Sabrina. I'm going to do it again, unfortunately. I've got a second lead on something financially suspect, and when I get back, we'll get into it. I know it's frustrating to give you little pieces of the puzzle, but I'm really feeling more hopeful about all this."

"Then I am too," Sabrina said supportively. "Thank you, always."

"You're welcome." She paused, and I could imagine a wry smile curling up a bit at her lips. "Is there any other important stuff you have for me that I should ignore for now? Because I have some news about your case."

I sat bolt upright in Ron's bed. "Why didn't you tell me?" I interrupted myself. "Oh, yeah, because I was talking nonstop. Okay. So, is it good or bad?"

Now it was Sabrina's moment to hesitate. "I'm not sure. It may just be a stupid clerical error that they haven't corrected and we just need someone to admit it and remove it."

"Well, that's the best news I've heard in a while. How'd you find out about this?"

"You know how I check the county's online database every morning under civil cases and it lists the divorce?"

"Right."

"So I guess I didn't have enough coffee in the morning because instead of the civil cases, I accidentally clicked on your case. As a criminal case."

"Wait a minute. Wait. I'll log onto their site with you." As I got out my laptop and anxiously waited to see the new details, Sabrina was already apologizing.

"Tyler, it may be nothing. And in a way, it doesn't make sense so…" She stopped talking, figuring correctly that I was trying to absorb the supposed criminal charges from the DA's office. I could feel my heart beating in my chest. I wondered, for a moment, if Sabrina could hear it pounding.

I repeated what I read in a hushed tone. "Eight counts of money laundering, theft and forgery." Each time I re-read it, my body grew more and more limp. How was this even possible?

Sabrina's voice was as tiny as she could make it. "It's a federal charge, in addition to a divorce. It's a RICO violation."

"Racketeering Influenced and Corrupt Organizations," I said, and the words sounded dire and intentional, no mistake at all.

"They messed up, right? We staff nursing homes, and they've got us mixed up with a bigger company. Right?'

"I don't know," I admitted. "Every white attorney I approached was willing to take my money to make this go away. They said they knew everyone at the DA's office, and then they all refused to help when they found out I've been stuck with a RICO charge. Which, by the way, they weren't really honest about, either."

"There must be some lawyer that could convince them?" Sabrina didn't seem sure, and she phrased it as a question, not a statement.

"Maybe some of them do," I reasoned, "but I doubt they're willing to sacrifice their careers to try and help me and risk making permanent enemies in Marietta."

"I feel so bad," Sabrina admitted. "Like I let you down."

"No, no, this fits," I said. "It could explain a lot about what Cindy was doing behind my back. Listen, I might be coming back tomorrow morning. I've got to confirm something with Ron, and then I'll call you at the office."

"Okay. I'll let you know if there are any status changes online."

I took a deep breath. "Sabrina, if you see anybody suspicious or get visited by anyone, just leave, go home. I'll find you there."

"Ty," she said smoothly, "I'll be in the office, holding down the fort, just like I always do. Bye."

I wandered in and out of sleep, too many possibilities crowding my mind. I worried about Shaun, my mom and Sabrina in Marietta and the inability to be there for them, day in and day out, if I was imprisoned. I dozed a little, but it was daybreak, and I wanted to make sure I had breakfast with Ron one last time, in case I had to leave West Palm Beach.

I listened carefully, and finally, I heard him get out of bed, turn on the water and get into a running shower. I opted for washing up and shaving, wondering, among the theories we'd been going through, which ones would stick with him. I quietly tiptoed downstairs, only to find Ron slowly boiling steel-cut oats, staring into the saucepan like a mystic.

"French roast?" Ron offered. I accepted, pouring it myself,

though that didn't take the sting out of being beaten to the kitchen once again.

"I tried to arrive downstairs first," I said lamely. I poured some creamer into the coffee, and the first gulp was like Heaven. I made a gurgling noise of approval.

"I appreciate your getting up early with me, anyway," Ron said. "Sleep okay?"

"Not really," I confessed, "but it wasn't the fault of the bed."

"Any more late-night revelations?" he joked, doling out the oatmeal and decoratively piling some strawberries on each of our bowls.

"I know it seems impossible, but yeah, there was a late-night call from Sabrina and what she told me might be as important as everything else I've learned."

I proceeded to recreate the whole cell phone call while Ron ate breakfast, his eyes glistening, taking in every detail but not saying a thing.

When I finished, I realized that I had been talking so much that I had only touched my coffee.

"What do you think?" I asked hesitantly. It mattered to me what his opinion was. Ron collected the dishes from both of us, washing them off and stuffing them into the dishwasher. He didn't answer at first. "Well?" I asked again.

"So it's a RICO violation…" He smirked.

"Exactly," I confirmed.

"Sounds more like a cocaine kingpin in Florida than a nursing home staff in Marietta. How would you even have access to that kind of money? Isn't it all wrapped up in insurance payments and Medicare?"

"Exactly. So, do you think Cindy knows somebody on the inside who—"

"All I know," Ron chimed in, "is that I should have been a private eye instead of a lawyer."

"Ron, I feel like you're not taking me seriously." He grabbed a jacket and some personal belongings and moved toward me. I started to stand to meet him.

"Sit down," he said. "I've got some stuff to say, and I want you to hear it."

"All right," I agreed, unsure why he seemed so upset.

"I don't know what exactly to think, but I do know one thing. Whatever happened, Cindy was damaged goods. She didn't deserve you, and I'm really fearful that you're going to pay a price for that. Now, I'll help you any way I can."

Ron started to walk to the front door. I quickly got up, eyes moist, and spun him around and hugged him with all my might.

"All right, then," Ron murmured. We separated from our bear hug. He dropped an extra pair of keys into my palm.

"Call me when you get the results from the clinic," he said. "And I will look into this RICO thing. It isn't my usual area, but I'll see what I can find. And maybe find a buddy who's licensed in Georgia, too." He was as choked up as I was and left quickly, before either of us could say the word "goodbye."

As I got into the city limits of Marietta, I called ahead to a local bistro and ordered a couple of gourmet meals, hoping Sabrina would like one of them.

"That's sweet," she said when she replied on our office phone, "but I picked up something earlier."

"Yeah, but was it bourbon-smothered pork chops or chicken-fried steak? It's still hot. Get out of that office. What do you say I bring you dinner at your house in fifteen minutes?"

"If I can have some of each," Sabrina asked. "As much as you want," I agreed.

A half hour later, Sabrina and I picked through the delicious remains of the food in her living room.

"I ate most of it," she replied a little guiltily.

"There's enough for another meal. I'll help you clean up."

"So, your discovery about the criminal charge might be the thing that breaks this open," I said hopefully. "We have to find out how a grand jury, directed illegally by someone at the DA, can deliver an indictment with no evidence, no bond posted and no notice given."

"It's a lot to figure out," Sabrina agreed. "Ron have any ideas?"

"A few. He's going to do some digging for me, too."

"Good." She smiled. "I'm glad you have friends looking out for you."

"So am I," I replied, silently praying that this would be over soon.

MISTAKE

I woke up on the couch at Sabrina's. It wasn't the first time, and we'd joked before that she needed a guest room for the times we stayed up late talking, but I was grateful for her support. Not everyone has a sister who cared this much, and I knew she had my back. It certainly didn't wipe out our legal problems—*my* legal problems—but knowing she believed in me gave me a little more confidence to solve the trap, the mistake, whatever it was that was lying in waiting for me.

I wished I could have kept her out of all this, but working in my office and being family, it was inevitable that she'd be involved. My heart would be hurt beyond measure to see Sabrina support me, only to have some false charge about our accounting laid upon her doorstep. I didn't know what the DA's office was capable of doing. I assumed it was worse than Sabrina even suspected. I could imagine her shock of a white sheriff threatening her with jail time if she did not supply purposely false testimony against me. And what would she do out of loyalty, in a horrible case like that? There was no telling, and the very thought of it deeply upset me.

I quietly washed up and tiptoed through the apartment,

successfully avoiding waking Sabrina. I was amused looking back at trying to beat Ron to the breakfast table at his house. I peeked into the refrigerator, and it seemed that everyone—Ron, Sabrina, my mama, my ex-wives—ate healthier than I did in my little pre-prepared, frozen food rental home. I helped myself to a small dish of fresh fruit salad from a larger bowl she had made and wrote a quick note to thank her for the support and let her know I'd see her at the office later.

It was just a bit past seven o'clock, and a low fog hung in the air. I was the only car on the street and began a left turn into the driveway alongside my apartment. That's when I saw the car, and I gasped for air, kicking the brake with my foot in a knee-jerk reaction. I rolled my eyes when I realized I was in the middle of the street. *Very conspicuous, Tyler.*

It wasn't a standard police car that was parked two spaces down from my door. It was a silver, late-model car with state license plates, and I knew as soon as I hesitated to turn into the drive, I'd been spotted. Dammit!

I continued entering the rutted dirt driveway, waiting to see if an officer would come out of the car. He did. He was in his forties, overweight, and he had one of his hands on a holstered gun, even though it would have been impossible to see more than my head and shoulders in the misty morning air. I slowly entered the driveway, stopped, jammed the car into reverse, roared back out into the street and squealed away in the direction I had come.

The cop looked astonished and lumbered back toward his vehicle and, I assumed, radioed in a report. I had no idea whether other police were spying on me in the neighborhood, but I did have a couple of advantages: I had lived my entire life in this town and began to cut down alleys and back roads to avoid any other officers. I heard the *screech* of the undercover officer's tires as he pursued, but there seemed to be no backup. I lost him in the minute and a half he was following me, and I evaded the main streets, peeking out at intersections until I was convinced I was not being followed.

My mother's car was parked halfway down its own driveway. I slowly maneuvered behind it, continuing slowly on the lawn until I reached a tool shed alongside her house. My heart was throbbing with fear. I entered the shed, its creaky doors making me even more nervous. I pulled out a tarpaulin, covered my car, draped some branches over it to make it seem like it hadn't been used in a while and sat alone in the musty shed, hoping no one would investigate.

After about a half hour, my mother's neighborhood began to wake up. Dogs were walking. Children were accompanied to bus stops. No one noticed the man behind the smeared glass in the tool shed, feeling like he was already imprisoned. I waited a half hour longer to call my mother, even though I knew she would be awake, puttering about. I didn't want to alarm her. I dialed her number from just outside the house.

"Honey, you got yourself your own key," she said, pleasantly surprised. "You know you're welcome any time. Come on in here."

My mother opened her mouth to question me, but I quieted her, put a comforting arm around her shoulder and walked her to the back door of the house. We exited, and I looked carefully around, but no one had noticed my hidden car. I explained what had happened with the undercover cop at my rental home. She lifted up the tarp and sadly looked at my car before quickly covering it up again.

"Such a nice-looking car," she mumbled. "I know how proud you are of it. It's a shame you got to hide it."

"Mama, I won't be here more than a couple days. Or I can stay with Sabrina. But I think I'm safer here for now. I guess the point is, they're coming after me. And they're close."

"You know already how I feel about it," she replied, leading me back into her house. "If they're dead set against providing you real justice, a real defense, then I guess you have to keep looking until you find that right person."

We were back in the kitchen. "You have anything to eat for breakfast?" she inquired. "Some, yeah," I answered, though my stomach growled.

"I'll make you a proper breakfast," she replied, smiling at me.

I went to my old bedroom, quietly shut the door and rang Sabrina. "You won't believe what just happened," I said, still shaken.

"What?"

"I got home and there was a cop at my house waiting for me. I hightailed it out of there."

"Oh my goodness! Are you okay?"

"Yeah, I'm at Mom's."

I could hear the relief in her voice. "Good, Mom's got you."

"Yeah, always."

"We can meet at the office to figure out what's next," Sabrina volunteered, refusing to give up, give in. I paused for a long time.

"Sabrina, it's very possible that this line is tapped. I'm going to call you later."

I knew that there was no certainty that the phone was tapped at the office, but it felt good anyway, in case law enforcement was listening, letting them know I knew they were dirty, they were corrupt and that I was not going down without a fight.

"Okay, I'm headed for the office," Sabrina confirmed. "I'll be there as soon as I can," I replied.

"Be careful."

As soon as I got off the phone, I was greeted with a swirling, magnificent array of aromas from my mother's kitchen. She was happily scurrying about, seemingly using every pot and pan, every oven and stove surface, and the griddle too.

"Mama," I said with a chuckle, "what are you making?"

"Everything!" she declared authoritatively, and I looked at her with a mixture of unshakable love and immense guilt, the latter of which I did my best to bury. It was easy to wipe the tears away and fool my mother into assuming that the moist eyes I had were about her generous cornucopia of food, lovingly prepared. That was true, but so was the dark, crawling idea inside my head that this was a last meal.

As I delighted in all the commingled tastes, she sat with me, insisted she had already had breakfast hours ago, and in between stories of my youth, she'd take a fork and cut off a sausage end, nibbling on it.

I borrowed my mother's car so I could use it to buy some cheap cell phones for important communications. I planned on going to the store after dinner. When I finished cleaning the last of my dishes, I felt a chill down my spine as goosebumps appeared along my arms, so I grabbed my jacket from the coat rack and bundled up. I felt the cold plastic of the pill bottle when I stuck my hand in the pocket for warmth. I had almost forgotten about those pills. My mind was feeling clearer these days. I still used the GPS while driving, but it was just for additional comfort. I knew what day it was, and what year it was too, and the bursts of Cindy memories were certainly arriving with more frequency. So now was the perfect time to "explore the puzzle," as Dr. Warren would say.

What had I not considered? When Cindy had locked me out and served the divorce papers, I had contacted every well-known attorney. One after the other, they seemed willing to represent me. Then, they found out that I had been charged criminally. Who would accept the likelihood of a RICO violation by a local businessman with a spotless record?

Well, any defense attorney who knew, for whatever reason, not to cross the DA on that particular case. Add to that no single Black defense attorney in Cobb County was even experienced in RICO violations, a federal offense. And it would make sense that Cobb County realized this and used it to their advantage. But, as evil as Cindy might have been, it made no sense for her to be associated with a criminal charge, although she was clearly ready to take every penny of mine, unfairly, in a shady divorce.

Or had she changed her mind? Was it possible Cindy was finally willing to discuss a settlement, with or without an attorney present? On a whim, I dialed Cindy, even though it was after eleven at night. I got her voicemail message.

"Cindy," I said, as professional and unbitter as possible. "Please, let's set up a meeting. We can't resolve things if we don't talk to each other. Thanks."

I hung up. I felt nothing, hearing her voice. I closed my eyes, tired of working on the puzzle. I wasn't sure how much later, but I seemed to hear something lightly scraping against the side of the house as I was dozing off on the couch. One of those late-night infomercials was running on the TV, and I had to mute the volume to make sense of the noises. Was it an animal? A bird maybe? I stood and paused near the front door for a moment. Cocking my head to the side, I listened intently. Oh no…it wasn't an animal. It was human voices I was hearing. Men, it sounded like a bunch of men. My instinct was to hide, but I stayed put, inching closer to the door. Was it just a noisy neighbor? I thought about waking Mama, but what good would that do? Suddenly, the volume of the voices grew louder. They must have been right on the other side of the wall.

"Do you wanna do the honors?" I heard a voice ask with perfect clarity.

My insides tumbled with an excruciating pang in my gut. I thought about looking through the peephole of the wooden door, but then I ran instead. Before I could make it to the bathroom, an explosion of wood and glass gave way to police in military uniforms, entering from both the front and rear doors. I was sandwiched by them on either side. I didn't even have time to blink.

My mother screamed, a loud and guttural wail. I ran into the bedroom and slammed the door as I yelled to her. Not a second later, three officers were bursting into my room. I sought protection in the corner by my lamp, but there was no escaping. They stalked me like prey as two grown men each grabbed one of my wrists and dragged my struggling body across the floor. I felt my back getting nicked by the wooden slabs beneath me as I screamed and shimmied, trying to get loose just so the pain would stop. But, of course, that's not what they wanted. They weren't thinking about my feelings, not even for a second, and especially not while they were taking turns beating me. I wasn't trying to be difficult. I was just in shock, but the officers were also highly aggressive.

Eventually, I stopped fighting. I stopped screaming, and I let my body go limp. That's when I noticed their handguns. They were enormous, and as soon as I laid eyes on them, the officers shoved them against my head, as if daring me to escape. But I had nowhere to go. I was surrounded.

"I will kill you, nigga!" more than one of them shouted, though I couldn't quite see who was talking. The blood drained from my head. I could feel it, trickling down my face and getting buoyed in my wrinkles. Everything started to blur as my vision dissolved into blackness. I began to lose consciousness. I prepared to let go of life.

REALIZATION AND RICO

Even if you have never visited a major county jail, there are things about it that don't require a great deal of imagination. You can fill in the horrific details of it based on seeing life within those walls depicted on television or film. In Cobb County Jail, there was, of course, an overabundance of Black prisoners compared to white ones. The conditions were as filthy and humiliating as I could stand. The walls needed re-painting, since every surrounding surface was covered in smears of God-knows-what. Dirt? Blood? Fecal matter? I didn't even want to know. The floors were scuffed and dusty, with random bits of litter piled in every hallway corner. There was also the smell, a combination of sweat and porta-potty. The surroundings, however, were less alarming than the people who lived within them.

You didn't have to talk to anyone to get a sense of the politics. The white gangs and Black gangs were clearly set, and one could also see which prisoners were looking forward to a day of release and which ones were in no hurry, because the crimes they committed guaranteed they would live behind bars a hopelessly long time. Everyone was incredibly readable.

Clearly, you don't have to be a felon to paint a picture of gang tattoos, homemade knives, rape, bribery with the guards, all of the disjointed, terrifying conditions I saw when I first arrived. The memory of stripping and coughing for the guard at the front desk will leave a permanent scar in my mind. So will the initial moments in my uniform.

When I walked into the lunchroom for the first time, I stared at my feet, hoping no one would notice the new face, but as soon as I looked up to find the end of the lunch line, I saw about a hundred pairs of eyes looking back at me, mostly glaring, taking me in. I closed my eyes, wishing I could pray myself away, but this was my new reality. At least I wasn't in the cell anymore. They practically pushed me into a cell with three other roommates, and when I offered a sheepish greeting, they all just stared at me before returning to their business. So I sat in my bottom bunk, closed my eyes, and said about twenty Hail Mary's to myself.

Some time, late at night, before I finally found some non-comforting sleep, I relived the no-knock assault on my mother's house—the raid that treated me like a murderous drug kingpin, not some guy who paid his taxes and was still beaten to a pulp. I had been an inch away from a white officer in a Kevlar vest shooting me in the face and likely telling his fellow officers and a board of inquiry later that I was trying to escape.

I thought that my circumstances could not have been any more nightmarish or bizarre.

It was very apparent I was being framed for a crime I did not commit, one for which police could readily find an excuse to kill a suspect, I realized. I didn't even know they could get a warrant for that—they must have had approval to enter my home without knocking, a No-Knock warrant I believe it's called. It was as if they wanted to catch me in the act, to blindside me while I was doing drugs or something, but I was only eating dinner with my mom.

None of it made any sense to me. I knew this meant that I had been framed, framed with evidence so substantial that it called for breaking and entering. But what was the evidence? What did they have on me?

I was pretty delirious when they told me my charges, but I did make out the word, *RICO*. "You are under arrest for a RICO violation. You have the right to remain silent," the tall white officer had recited as he'd cuffed me. I can't remember what happened after that, but I remember how sweaty the officer's hand felt against my wrist—a testament to all the energy he exerted while beating the shit out of me. In order to burst through my house and arrest me on the spot like that, they must have had a judge's signature. They must have had legitimate reason to send me here, or at least a legitimate-looking lie. And now I was isolated in a cell alone, my body battered by the assault team, despite the fact that I was not overly muscular or aggressive in nature. And the last piece of the puzzle, at least for the other prisoners who observed me, was a final question: why was this guy, thrashed half to death, given his own cell *right next to death row?*

If Cobb County's intention was to terrify and intimidate me, they were going overboard. I didn't know how they came up with the charges, and there was no way to get out of jail because there was no bail bond, which I thought was illegal. And before and after I left my cell each day, I glanced into the eyes of those men who had no hope of a full life. I stood my ground but said little to anyone, which I suppose made me, the black-and-blue new guy, a real curiosity.

The two rival gangs, the Crips and the Bloods, who grew out of the rivalry in '90s South Central Los Angeles, made comments about me as a curiosity. "Hey, check out Elon over there. He thinks he's so much better than us," I overheard one of the taller inmates say while walking past me during lunch hour.

They seemed to think that I was a businessman, a guy who might be able to make them money after they were released. I later realized "Elon" was a nickname taken from Elon Musk. Although I kept to myself, I could tell people found me confusing, but I was just as confused about my own position in this community. Like why the hell I was there.

I didn't want to communicate with anyone because I feared it would indicate I was on one side or the other. But I also knew that after a time, this would be unavoidable, even if I did nothing. One afternoon, on my third day as an inmate, I was out in the yard, sitting by myself, trying to appear invisible. Two Crips gang members walked up to me and around me, as if studying a strange animal in a zoo.

The first Crip observed, "Man, they look like they messed you up pretty bad, homie."

The second suggested, "He's lucky he's alive." Then he directed his attention toward me. "You shot anybody?"

I wondered how much to tell, how crazy it might sound. Then again, sounding crazy might be enough to get prisoners to leave me alone. I started out briefly, saying I was wrongly arrested for a RICO violation even though all I did for a living was staff nursing homes. The two gang members snapped to attention when I mentioned "RICO" and were fascinated by this miscarriage of justice and asked more questions until we had to leave the yard.

The next day, the two Crips brought some of their friends to hear about the guy almost murdered in his mother's house and never even given a formal charge, but they backed off about fifty feet before they approached because a group of their sworn enemy had already surrounded me. There were about six or seven Bloods in a semi-circle, listening, throwing out questions. I figured that the only way to talk about what had happened to me was with an attitude of defeat, not one of bragging or righteous anger or even disgust against a racist system.

As I answered questions from them, their fury, their cursing, their sense of the impossibly unjust took over. I was sure that many of those gangbangers had killed or maimed others, but when they responded to my simple, unvarnished story of being taken down, being crushed, even after obeying the law, I felt the weight of their lives, their fatal previous decisions to give up and get what they could while they could.

So, for the time being, there were the Crips, there were the Bloods, GDs and Muslims, then there was me—the Black, middle-class no man's land of unjustified crime.

One day, I was in line to call Sabrina to check for an update. As I got ready to make my call, which cost a dozen times more than a direct call, a small, nervous, skinny-looking Blood cut in line. I made the mistake of simply saying, "I'm next."

The Blood clearly knew I would back down, and his cursing me and facing me, ready for a confrontation, made it even more apparent. I was willing to give way, especially when I saw the gleam of a handmade knife lifted partially from the pocket of his prison jumpsuit. I had avoided gang warfare for weeks, and now, pathetically, I saw myself getting shanked by a kid without enough sense to realize I was letting him cut in front of me.

A chorus of angry voices seemed to drive the Blood toward the inevitable decision to plunge the blade into me. There were no guards in sight. I looked around and hoped one would show up in time. Then, another Blood who had heard my story in the yard shouted above the others, "He didn't cut in on you!" to his fellow gangster. "Man, this is the guy they framed who finds staff for the nursing homes. So back the fuck off!"

That provided the extra time for guards to arrive, barking at everyone, asking what was going on and predictably, not getting any answers from anyone. From then on, I had no trouble with gangs, But I wasn't getting any closer to getting a bail bond or legal representation.

Work details, like most everything else in Cobb County, were guided by color lines. Certainly, the gangs were separated, and the whites—obviously racist and separatist—were prevented from working anywhere near Crips and Bloods. Hispanic gangs were more powerful in the other areas of the country, but there was a gang present at Cobb too.

My work assignment was lifting boxes of frozen food from a storage facility and moving it to a freezer for later use in cooking for the prisoners. There were two lines of prisoners moving those boxes, Crips and whites. We were visible at times by one another, but we did not talk to each other and that was intended. Still, some of the other white prisoners found out about me and wondered about my federal raid on a RICO charge, no bail, living a middle-class life before everything turned upside down for me. I saw some of these white convicts look me in the eye and want to question me, but my being surrounded by gang members of my own race convinced them it wasn't worth the risk of being confronted or thrown into solitary confinement for allegedly starting a fight.

But I couldn't continue to live off of my savings indefinitely. I hated asking for help, but lately, I'd found that I had no choice. I only got access to one phone call about every two days, so I made it a point to plan these calls strategically. First, I called my mom, just to make sure she knew everything was okay. It didn't feel right to ask her for money, so I decided against it. Really, I just enjoyed listening to her voice, until the inevitable crying started, of course. I hated hearing her cry, hated that I was the source of her sadness.

Sometimes I wondered if she really believed me, if she really believed in my innocence. But those kinds of thoughts were pointless, unproductive.

My calls with Sabrina were way more business-like. My last conversation with her—whether it was tapped or not—was a discussion about my bank account waning, due to the travel I had done, as well as maintaining the office, Sabrina's salary and other family obligations. I didn't need a lot of money to survive in jail, just enough for toothpaste, snacks, all of the essentials...but with everything being so uncertain, I did wish I had more money, just for the sake of security. I mentioned this to Sabrina, and she said she was going to sell some of her clothes so she could send me an extra check. That made my head pound. I didn't want her doing any more for me than she already *was* doing.

And I was very paranoid of people listening in on our phone calls. I felt like they, someone, was waiting for the right moment when I was desperate and confused enough to accept a deal—any deal. And then I received valuable legal advice from the unlikeliest of sources.

We had breaks built into our jobs, and I was not big on talking to my fellow prisoners. So I would find a corner near the freezer we were filling, sit on a couple of empty boxes and close my eyes, seeing myself somewhere else, with family or friends, living out the life I should have had.

"Hey, buddy. Can I talk to you for a minute?"

I opened my eyes. A white convict, about forty-five, with a grey-and-brown-streaked beard, was looking around nervously, then at me.

"Listen, I want to help you. I know about that raid. That's what Cobb County does when they can't get you for anything else." I looked around. Both of us were taking a risk, but he seemed to have knowledge, and I had nothing to lose.

"Tyler," I introduced myself with a whisper. "Lamont." He did the same.

"What did you mean: Cobb County creates a new charge when they can't get you otherwise?"

"I'm telling you, it happened to my buddy. He was a businessman, just like you." Lamont drew in two steps closer, putting more urgency in his voice.

"My buddy fought it. Same thing happened. They made it a RICO charge. Minimum twenty years and wiped him out financially." My mind reeled.

"Do you know the name of the DA?"

"Naw, but the lot of them fuckers is corrupt. There's no way of winning against them."

"I assume your friend was white?" I asked.

"Yeah. Listen, man, no offense to you, but how many defense lawyers in Cobb County are willing and able to fight the DA and are Black?"

"Zero," I replied instantly, and he nodded. "And no white lawyer will go up against them either."

"I know," Lamont admitted. "They decide what the law is."

"Maybe they already saw my wife was suing for divorce and they figured—"

"A little more pressure and you'd cave in," Lamont concluded.

"So, what am I supposed to do?" I asked desperately. "Well, don't take this the wrong way..."

"Just say it, okay?"

"You can't get any white lawyer in Cobb to help, so you got to use a Black public defender."

I sighed, exasperated. "They don't have any power. They've got dozens of cases, and they're there to lessen the sentence and that's it."

Lamont and I held each other in our gaze for a long time. Then, from far off, we heard a guard yell out, "Break's over. Back to work."

"They got one bit of power, Tyler." Lamont was already moving off. "Instead of twenty years, maybe they'll get you ten years. Or even five." And he was gone, before I could thank him or even find out what he himself was charged with.

I thought, when I eventually learned what was happening to me, there would be a small sense of relief. That's not to say that I would have a solution for my troubles. But I felt that when the day came that

I knew what I was up against, I could begin to make a plan to attain justice. Instead, I felt like my legs had been cut out from under me.

The following day, I sat in a windowless room at Cobb County Jail for what seemed like forty-five minutes. I didn't know who I was waiting for—I just knew that I was supposed to meet someone. There were four additional tables set up, scattered across the room. Each one had an inmate sat at them, waiting, just like me. I watched as a few of their guests trickled in: an old woman with a floral scarf who dabbed her eyes with her index finger upon entering, a man in his thirties who smiled like he had just won the lottery when he shouted, "Paul! Hi!" before running to the table behind me. I stared at the soda machine straight ahead as I listened to the muffled conversations around me. This went on long enough for me to forget why I was even sitting there.

Finally, a man in his forties, wearing a suit, entered. He wore a smirk more than he did a smile, and he seemed to enjoy analyzing me, judging me. I knew that I had very little on my side at that point: a Black man falsely accused of crimes, not given due process, likely with an entire county legal organization willing to back up any charge, no matter how unlikely or absurd.

I had the truth on my side, and though many a man has been executed for deeds he had not done, I decided to let this person know I was aware how utterly corrupt his office was, even without a plan for justice. They had beaten me, threatened to kill me, called me the most hateful language they could think of. I would figure out strategy later. Now, it was time to say, *I'm a man. You're not. You're not even human.*

"Tyler, do you know who I am?"

I looked at his smug face. How would I know who he was? I didn't even know why I was being charged with a felony to begin with. Based on his demeanor, though, it didn't seem like this was an attorney Sabrina might have sent. The way this guy sat back in his chair when he talked to me, sizing me up, didn't read as very lawyer-like.

"I'd like to know."

"I'm James Marvin, assistant DA, Cobb County. I'm handling your case."

"You realize that filing false criminal charges and not granting a bail bond are illegal in the United States, right?" I felt I needed to cut right to the chase.

"Your current, soon-to-be ex-wife has filed both civil charges, namely divorce, as well as the RICO violation this office is pursuing."

"Proof of which you have not provided, prompting my being beaten, unarmed, naked, opening up your office to a civil law suit at the very least. And while we're at it—"

"While we're at it," Marvin interrupted me, "what's the name of your attorney again?" He paused, enjoying the moment. "Oh, that's right. You don't have one. Because you can't get one. You can get a public defender. Maybe even a Black one. And the judge you've been assigned will gladly follow our guidelines for each charge. Which will be twenty years a piece. And testimony about your character and your financial violations will be provided by your soon-to-be ex-wife Cindy. *With whom I am currently engaged in a sexual relationship.*"

I wasn't sure I'd heard him right at first. Sexual relationship? I repeated the words to myself before repeating them out loud again. "Sexual relationship? Is that what you just said?"

"You heard me right. I'm the guy sharing a bed with Cindy these days. Bet you didn't see that coming, huh?"

I squeezed the skin on my forehead, just above my eyes, folding my wrinkles into each other as I let Marvin's words sink in. I wanted to stand up, but then I noticed the glare from the guard in the corner of the room. He was staring at me, as if he knew my adrenaline was pumping at an all-time high. For the past few days, I'd watched angry men cope with their rage unsuccessfully. I'd been the victim of a random shanking. I'd seen someone punch a wall. And just yesterday, I'd watched someone throw a plate across the room because the ketchup ran out.

I considered myself a gentle soul, someone with a long fuse, but right now, wearing handcuffs in a room full of criminals with guards ready to pounce, I felt that I could metamorphose into someone I wasn't. I could be that aggressive, masculine stereotype that ran rampant in prisons like this. I could hop on this table and strangle Marvin with the very cuffs that kept my hands restricted. He deserved it, after all. And I wouldn't feel bad about it. I could give him a head injury worse than mine. Maybe Cindy would grow resentful toward him just like she did with me after the fall. But as the blood coursed through me, I studied Marvin's face. The shape of his eyes reminded me of my therapist's, but maybe that's just because I was angry at him too, for saying Cindy was sexually adventurous.

"Are you jealous?" Marvin interrupted my thoughts to ask, but I was still thinking about what my therapist had said. This is just who Cindy was. This smug asshole sitting in front of me was just another victim. Another toy for Cindy's amusement. I took a deep breath, in through my mouth and out through my nose. Finally, I responded.

"Jealous? I feel bad for you."

"I'm not the one in handcuffs," he responded a second later, like he'd been waiting to say that. I chuckled to myself, disgusted. "Something funny about all this, Tyler?"

"Ironic, you might say."

Marvin leaned on the back of the chair tucked into the desk. "So, here's what you're going to do, Tyler. Cindy tells me you have about seventy-five thousand dollars left on hand. You are going to give her that, which she has generously agreed to split with me."

I stared him down, making him wait for my answer. "You know that you're corrupt, and you know that Cindy is too. So, I will grant everything I own to Cindy in a divorce, which is worth more than seventy-five thousand dollars in value. In exchange, you drop these false charges against me, and I wish the two of you good luck." I murmured as an afterthought, "You're going to need it."

"No, Tyler, you are going to give us that money, and then we will go on with the criminal and civil cases."

"Tell me something, James Marvin. Was this all your idea, or was it Cindy's?"

Marvin was now looking annoyed, having expected an answer right away. "That doesn't matter because my boss, the DA, and the judge will give you multiple sentences of twenty years if you don't agree."

"It's interesting," I said, "that a man like you can break the bonds of holy matrimony, as well as the laws of the United States without a single moment to consider what your *soul* is worth. By the way, an attorney I spoke with told me you're also a pastor of a church.

Cindy once mentioned being involved with the pastor of her church. I figure that's where you and Cindy started your affair."

Marvin cleared his throat, upset but still in control of his emotions. "As a matter of fact, Tyler, I am a pastor at a church, and I will pray that you do the right thing." He quickly left the room.

As two guards on either side of me marched me back to my cell, I recalled a memory, flashing back to Cindy, tearfully lying to me. She had said that she'd had an affair in the past with a pastor, making it sound like she had been manipulated and heartbroken in the process.

I realized, as the cell door swung open, that Cindy had been seeing James Marvin before she'd even met me, and she had likely never stopped.

GOODBYE MARIETTA

Now that Marvin had admitted his affair with Cindy, I wanted to propose to her the deal that Marvin wouldn't accept. Logically, they both wanted to put me away forever. I was an ongoing threat to them. But Cindy knew me better, and if she sensed that I would not budge from my position, she just might try to take everything in the divorce and drop the false charges. She was, I now knew, amoral and criminal. I had to find out if she was totally unreasonable as well. I was looking forward to leaving a message for Cindy, even though I was sure she wouldn't have the courage to talk directly to me. I wanted to feel the satisfaction of both calling her a liar and knowing she was one, even though there would be no reply on the phone.

After completing my first month in Cobb, I found that although I'd only had a few conversations with inmates, there seemed to be a significant number of men, mostly Black but also white and Hispanic, who nodded my way, as if to say, "We know you don't belong here." I returned their silent acknowledgments with subtle bows of my head, and it gave me more conviction when I waited my turn to use the phone to confront Cindy. I never explained my whole story to any of the other guys. I didn't want to divulge too much information when I still had so many questions about my charges. But I did tell Taco about my situation with Cindy while lifting weights a few nights ago.

I don't think Taco was his real name, but it's what he introduced himself as, and I didn't want to pester him with questions about it. Taco was a talker, and after telling me a long-winded story about his ex-girlfriend setting his truck on fire, I felt comfortable enough to confide in him about the affair. So I told him about Cindy's bathroom phone calls, my fall, and Marvin showing up unannounced to confirm the cheating.

"Damn, son," Taco acknowledged. "That's some calculated bullshit."

I laughed at that, so much that my diaphragm cramped. It felt great to really laugh. For the first time in a long time, I finally felt seen by someone. Taco's dumb and simple acknowledgment of my fucked-up life made me feel more whole somehow, more able to continue fighting this whole thing with conviction.

I smiled to myself as I reflected on Taco's words, standing there with the cold plastic of the payphone rubbing against my ear. I listened to the phone dialing, hoping, praying she'd pick up with each passing ring, but then her outgoing voicemail message played, and I squeezed my eyes shut.

"Cindy, it's Tyler in Cobb County Jail. James Marvin of the DA's office just told me that you and he are having a sexual affair." Really, it had been several weeks since I'd learned of the affair, and I only now had the courage to confront Cindy about it, but she didn't have to know that. I wanted this voicemail to sound urgent. "Before you erase this message, consider saving it because Marvin said some things about you that you might need for your eventual defense."

I waited a couple beats.

"Let's see…I've got notes here on what he said. Well, I figure he was telling the truth about you cheating on me, which means you're both involved in filing a false divorce suit. And a pastor, Cindy? Like the one you told me you stopped seeing years ago? Did you stop? Anyway, Marvin also tried to extort seventy-five thousand dollars which you and he plan to split. Now, you're into federal crimes, Cindy. And you still intend to divorce me on some fake financial charges. Or is it just Marvin's greedy idea to get seventy-five thousand dollars out of me? And is he really sharing that amount with you? Did you even know about the money?"

I took another five seconds to let all of that sink in. "It's my mistake that I married you, Cindy. I accept my responsibility in that. I'll lie for you and your affair, and you can have everything in the divorce. But you better get him to drop the charges for the RICO violation. Because if he won't, I've got nothing to lose. And I'm coming after you both, legally. The Governor's office. The Prosecuting Attorney's office. The Georgia Bureau of Investigation. The Georgia Bar Association. And no matter what happens to Marvin, there's more than enough to end your career as a doctor, Cindy. I'm offering you a chance to take everything I own *except my freedom*, Cindy. Is this worth it? Decide soon and let me know."

Cindy never called me back, which wasn't surprising, but it was clear that after my phone message, she and Marvin had a discussion about how to handle me and my threats. They didn't seem too worried about my going after them through the state government. But Marvin did finally see to it there was a bond, which I posted, expensive and corrupt as it was. I was informed just a week after I recorded that voicemail for Cindy. Marianne at the front desk told me it would cost $80,000 to see the outside world again. All the breath nearly left my body as she explained my new bond status. I almost wanted to hug her, but I still wasn't sure if $80,000 was doable. As she was yammering about bond procedures, I was mentally calculating how much I might receive for selling my car. I could ask Sabrina to sell it for me. I just needed to get her the registration somehow.

I didn't want to get my hopes up, but when I relayed the news to Sabrina on the phone that afternoon, she was more ecstatic than I was. "Don't worry, Tyler. We'll make this work. I'm gonna call your mom right now. Don't worry. This is great news."

I repeated those words to myself for the remainder of the night: *This is great news. This is great news.* For the first time since being in prison, I may have something to look forward to.

For my troubles, I received an electronic ankle monitor, assuring the police and court system that I wouldn't leave Cobb County. I celebrated my newly won and hard-fought freedom by having Sabrina and Shaun join me and my mother for a home-cooked meal, which she insisted on making, despite my offering to take us all to any restaurant they wanted.

In addition to copies of papers I filed, I kept duplicates hidden in a safe in my home. I filed the formal complaints I threatened I would over the phone to Cindy. And although I never saw him again, the white convict at Cobb County, Lamont, clearly knew what he was talking about: the Cobb County DA's office, whether it was just Marvin or others, was using RICO statutes to extort prisoners—in my case, *innocent* prisoners—for profit. I had to try and reach out to lawyers in Fulton County.

I made appointments with attorneys in and around Atlanta, those who seemed to have the power and expertise to fracture the racist power base in Cobb County. Every male and female lawyer who I chose in Fulton County replied, although many of them said they wanted to save me an unnecessary drive on I-75 South. Their responses were different combinations of what I already knew. As an example, one said, "Cobb County is a racist and closed community that does what it likes despite the rest of the state. And if you bring in someone from Fulton County, they're all going to band together and attack. They'll treat your attorney like he or she comes from California, not Atlanta."

I expected this kind of reply, knowing it was true, but I was crushed because everyone in Fulton agreed, feeling there was no point in even battling the rot within the system. I managed to get two attorneys to set dates to meet with me, more out of pity than an actual plan to deal with the powers that be in Cobb County.

I got the second lawyer to meet me at a Carrabbas, which was walking distance from Sabrina's. She arrived early, waiting in her booth with the menu propped up as I meandered over. When her eyes finally met mine, her eyebrows furrowed like she was taking me in, although it was hard to decipher whether she was judging me or the menu items.

Regardless, I was happy she was giving me her time.

"Hi, Francis," I muttered as I approached her, extending my hand, which she shook with confidence

"Hi, Tyler."

She was one of the only female attorneys in the area, appointed to a circuit court judge. She looked very guilty and uncomfortable nibbling around a huge bowl of pasta as I summarized what had happened and tried to come up with alternate solutions.

Finally, overcome by disgust, Francis tossed down her fork in rage. "Tyler, everyone on the inside of Georgia politics knows how RICO has been misused. We have no New-York-style mobsters. We wouldn't think of doing what Cobb does, but they don't answer to the federal government. James Marvin and the people who protect him are in this for profit. Nobody is going to say, "I'm innocent even though I can't prove it, so I don't care if you keep tacking on twenty-year minimum sentences."

"But that's just it," I insisted. "Marvin is out of control. He wants to clean out my bank account in exchange for nothing. Cindy will get everything in the divorce, and they'll still give me the maximum sentence."

Since leaving jail, I'd been able to track my finances more

easily, and I knew Marvin was responsible for my account's sudden depletion. He'd also made a habit of sending aggressive text messages under a pseudonym. The past three days in a row, I'd woken up to messages like, "You're going down," sent from a random number. Clearly, Marvin had a lot of time on his hands.

"No, they won't," she assured me, "but I wouldn't blame you for saying ten years is a much better deal for being innocent of your crimes than thirty or forty years."

"There has got to be a way around this." I hurled the napkin onto the table.

"Well, I've only just learned about your case, but if you wanna start with a fair stipend, I'll keep working on it. Maybe two hundred dollars for the week? How does that sound?" she offered.

"Sure, as long as you think you can help."

"Oh yeah, I know these Marvin types like the back of my hand. I'd like to help you." I smiled. "Thank you."

"But in the meantime, pick a public defender in Cobb that is as sympathetic as you can find, and work out what you want and what the judge is likely to give you. And I'm sorry to say it, Tyler, but even though you're clearly a model citizen, the DA and judge will treat you like the Crips and Bloods in Cobb County Jail."

I asked Sabrina for her opinion. I already knew our mother's attitude: if the state of Georgia wanted to rob her of her son's remaining freedom, she wanted to fight back with everything she had, fists and fingernails. But Sabrina was a bit more practical. She had more knowledge of the financial side of things, and I thought she might hesitate at the idea of putting more money into lawyers' pockets, but when I reported all the details after my dinner with Francis, her eyes sparkled with hope.

"I feel good about this," she admitted. "I trust a woman's advice on this one."

I felt inclined to soak in a bit of her optimism. Holding back my tears, I clasped her hands between mine in appreciation and made plans to choose the most motivated Black public defender for Cobb County.

This was a relatively easy task because a guy named Cooper was the only Black court-appointed defense in the entire county. Cooper was tall, skinny and wore thick eyeglasses. His pupils became enormous during our initial discussion. When I told him that I wanted to plea myself innocent before the judge, that I wanted to fight for my well-deserved freedom, Cooper looked nauseated, as if he was more concerned with his dead-end job prospects than my limited future outside a cell.

Although Sabrina trusted Francis, we had our doubts about Cooper. She warned me before I went to talk to him, "Remember everything he says and study his body language. We can't risk being manipulated by another guy trying to earn a quick buck."

That's how I found myself in Cooper's cramped office with duct tape glued to my rib cage wrapped around a recording device. It blinked green under my button-down, but Cooper couldn't see that.

"What do you mean, you want to go to trial? I guarantee you that the judge will take their recommendation and give you thirty years!"

"What about a trial? What about justice? What about the history of corruption in this office, Cooper? Don't you feel responsible to fight against that?"

"You're crazy," Cooper shot right back in a hushed voice. "What world are you living in? You pay Marvin the money he wants, and you hope the judge gives you a major break."

"Wait a minute. You *know* Marvin is extorting me for seventy-five thousand dollars?"

"Of course I know. I'm trying to help you. If you don't agree to give up the seventy-five thousand, then at least enter a guilty plea. If you don't do either of those things, I am telling you that you will likely get thirty years. Do you understand that?"

"I understand clearly how justice works here, Cooper, and what part *you* play."

When I got back to the office, I removed the miniature digital recorder that Sabrina had taped to my chest.

"Sorry about the hair loss," she apologized after ripping the tape off my midsection. "Was my idea worth it?"

"I think so, but I'll let you tell me. Let's give it a listen."

I rewound the tape and randomly played it. Cooper's voice could be clearly heard, saying, *"If you don't do either of those things, I am telling you that you will likely get thirty years."*

"Well done," I complimented Sabrina. "You could work for the GBI."

"I already have a good job. Family business, you know." She laughed.

"Well," I joked, "thank goodness you have a nice boss. We'll send a copy of this ANDA letter to the Georgia Bar Association and see what they think about the DA's office in Cobb County."

I sent the letter registered with a return receipt. I followed up twice a week with anyone who could have possibly signed for it. Every Tuesday and Thursday, I'd wake up and dial the Association office while my coffee maker sputtered fresh caffeine. Sometimes, the calls were more productive than other times. It totally depended on who answered, and how much time and knowledge they had. So I made sure to keep calling religiously, which I did for about four weeks. After week three, nearly everyone in the office knew me by name. No one admitted to seeing the letter. I had every suspicion that the Governor and the GBI were not going to act upon the dirt going on in their administration, but the Georgia Bar Association was a shock, a wake-up call, suggesting that I was so far out of my league in fighting the battle that I had only begun to realize how hopeless my case was.

It was now forty-one days until my court date, and I felt a bit like

Jesus when he spent forty days and nights alone in the desert. All I could do was keep walking, keep surviving and keep holding on to my faith. It felt like each passing week brought a flurry of good and bad news simultaneously, until it was hard to distinguish whether or not I had a right to feel positive. Today, for the first time in a few weeks, I was beginning to feel hopeless. I sank lower and lower into a depression, and I hadn't really prepared how to explain to Shaun how he was living in a society that had different rules for people of different skin color. I feared all the positive messages and love I had given him throughout his childhood would be tossed away, no longer worth believing.

It wasn't that I was afraid he would no longer love me, as his father. It was an inner knowledge that I wanted to protect him from the dangers and poisonous thoughts of this world. And not only had I failed to show him how to stand up to those evils, but also, even more horrendous, I had fallen prey to them. What kind of example was I setting?

That meant that the people closest to me could not count upon me anymore to help them in any little way I could. My going to prison, possibly for the rest of my life, was proof that my best intentions for them, their dreams and hopes, were pointless. And there was another realization, as I sank lower, unable to respond to Sabrina or my mother and their attempts at positivity, for a solution that still would be found. My life, my education, my country had failed me. That was a special kind of hurt, because there was no other country I wanted to be from. Patriotism is a deep faith in the righteousness and goodness of your nation, and now, issues like slavery and the battle for civil rights and use of force in shootings of Black men and women by white officers were not going to be arguments around a table. They were going to be a history that was greeted every morning, along with iron bars.

Sabrina was the only one who suggested that the pills I had been given by Dr. Warren could still be of some use. I had stopped seeing him since I left town, but I still had the pill bottle he gave me in my nylon bag of toiletries. I hadn't heard from Dr. Warren since he left a voicemail about three months ago, asking if I planned on coming in for my regularly scheduled appointments. I never called back, but I did think about Dr. Warren around once a day, sometimes feeling thankful for his help, and other times, feeling bitter about his lack of understanding. Obviously, I had, as they say, lingering "issues" with Dr. Warren, and now that I had found out more about Cindy's lies and behavior, I felt even more entitled to reject his pills that numbed me, that tranquilized me. But now, with the prospect of prison for decades stretching out ahead of me, I thought about those pills, about how my anxiety and sense of failure might in fact benefit from some of those drugs.

Still, I kept going back and forth in my mind about the remaining days of freedom.

Didn't I owe my family the real me instead of a drugged-out shell of a person? But that made no sense either, because my last days of freedom, without Dr. Warren's pills, were going to be a depressed, guilt-ridden version of me with little to say, and I also did not want to be remembered like that. And was there a possibility that taking the pills again would somehow influence my decision to allow a plea and shave some years off my sentence? I didn't know anymore if that was the wrong or right decision.

Now that there seemed to be no chance to be free again unless I gave everything away to the DA, to Marvin and Cindy, what was I fighting for anymore? That central question haunted me as I had my last pre-trial meeting with Cooper in his office, the day before surrendering myself and entering a plea. I had been walking around like a ghost the whole week prior, mumbling to everyone who cared about me. I had made no decisions, and even worse, I hadn't had the courage to ask others what I should do, if I should change my mind.

And then, hunched over, only half listening, half arguing with myself in my head, I heard Cooper say, "We know the judge, Margaret Bell Haden. She almost always takes the suggestion of the prosecutor. Unless you both change your plea and agree to the seventy-five thousand, it's almost certain to be thirty years."

Cooper stared at me across the long, cherry wood table, trying to read my expression, but I don't think he had much success. The lights in his office were so bright that I did feel vulnerable, naked almost, but I had become an expert at masking my true feelings when need be. This whole situation made me a better liar, which I found ironic since I only wanted to reveal the truth. There are no generally accepted expressions of agreement or denial when it comes to madness. I believe as desperate and confused as I was, I didn't make the decision until the last words I heard from Cooper, which funnily enough, he used to counsel me about family.

"Tyler, please, do this for your relatives. In ten or fifteen years, your mother will still be here. Shaun will likely be married and maybe have kids of his own. And you can get to know them—on the *outside of prison*. Think about—Tyler? Where are you going?"

I don't remember leaving him or getting in my car or parking outside of Cooper's office. I do remember thinking it would be too painful to have a conversation with anyone. I looked around on the street. Marietta went on, its people having places to go. I closed my eyes and created a mental picture of everyone I'd loved and who'd loved me, faces I may not see in the flesh for years to come. I had a choice to make. I could either plead guilty, despite my innocence, and earn a possible future with the people I love, many, many years from now, or I could plead innocent and hope the judge saw me for who I really am. I knew I was innocent, but it wasn't that simple. Would pushing for my innocence just sabotage me in the end? Even though it was the truth? Would my stubbornness be the thing to keep me from spending time with Shaun out in the real world?

It was all too much to think about, the stakes unnervingly high. So instead of ruminating any further, I rolled down the driver's side window and took in the radiance of the blue sky. I uncapped a water bottle. I waited until two businessmen walked by. Then, I began to alternate large handfuls of Dr. Warren's pills with slugs of water. When the pills were gone, I slumped back in the car seat. The last thing I felt was a cool breeze on my cheek, like a light kiss.

PLANNED CRUELTY

My eyelids were not completely raised, but still, the overhead lights were too bright.

There was a sharp, nauseating antiseptic smell to the air. I heard a woman in the distance moaning over and over. It was incomprehensible, but she continued, though thankfully not too loudly, as if it was a prayer she held sacred and dear. I carefully opened my eyes slowly, taking in the pale green ceiling and walls of the hospital, a green that suggested bile or leakage of a vital organ. And then my eyes focused upon Sabrina and my mother, who were growing more animated with every waking flutter of my eyelids.

"He's alive!" Sabrina said triumphantly, and while I appreciated her love and dedication, I couldn't share her enthusiasm for still being here. When I was awake and alive, I thought about my future, about all the possible scenarios and various ways my life could implode even worse than it already had. My only solace was sleep, and a part of me still hoped that I could go to sleep forever.

"Thank the Lord for keeping him with us!" my mother exclaimed, and she clasped her hands together in appreciation and triumph.

I had been conscious no more than a minute, but I felt worse than before I contemplated that mound of Dr. Warren's pills that had been in my hand. I wasn't selfish enough to not consider how my suicide would cause pain for the people in my life, but I calculated that it would fade, and that on the other hand, my presence behind bars, year after year, would generate a particular kind of suffering for the family.

Now, there was another level of shame connected to my story, but in the moment, the two most important women to me were tearfully happy. My thoughts were jumbled. Someone had used some kind of tube to suck the pills from my stomach, and my throat was raw. I tried to speak but couldn't manage any words.

"Get him some water," my mother advised, "so he can speak." She and Sabrina adjusted the bed and poured some water in a plastic cup with a straw. I cautiously drank and thought how anything I said would be insufficient.

"I'm so sorry," I managed to croak, and sure enough, they instantly forgave my idea to try to take my life, while I was still ashamed of it.

"We've got to contact Cooper right away," Sabrina said.

While my mother tried to reach Cooper, Sabrina explained that while I was in the hospital, I would miss the trial date that was already set. "The doctors said you need to stay here for another three days at least. And your trial is exactly three days from now. I've been talking to Cooper at least once a day." Her voice trailed off at the end of her sentence, like she didn't want to disturb me, but before she could continue, my mother motioned the room to silence, as she finally got Cooper to come to the phone.

"Cooper," my mother insisted, "Tyler is going to be okay. He survived. We need to set a new court date for him."

She listened to his reply over the phone, and her disturbed reaction told me everything about Cooper and his attitude about me going to prison.

"But he's recovered and he's here at the hospital. He's not a fugitive. It's not—"

My mother stopped talking as Sabrina and I sadly looked over at her. It appeared he had hung up on her. She looked at her cell phone, as if it was some slimy kind of creature, pressed a button and returned it to her purse.

"That's crazy. These people are just plain crazy."

"What did he say?" asked Sabrina.

I didn't want to know. I figured that Cooper no longer cared if I spent the rest of my life in jail, whether I had broken any laws or not.

"He said that they wrote out a warrant for Tyler's arrest and sent it to the judge. Even though Tyler's in this hospital." My mother sat on the edge of the bed next to me. "What kind of people are we dealing with?" she asked.

"I'm not sure they're human beings," Sabrina said, her words biting.

I reached out and held them both. With a raw-sounding voice, I managed to say, "I'm sorry I messed things up, but I'm glad I can still see you, no matter what."

My maintaining my status as innocent, even to the degree that I was willing to take my life, did not impress either Cooper or the judge in charge of my case. She issued a warrant for my arrest, even though I was not about to leave the hospital in my condition.

The administration of the hospital confirmed that I was suicidal but not a threat to others, that my depression about being sentenced without proper representation was the clear cause of my actions. I knew this because a letter arrived at the hospital that Sabrina shared with me once I felt coherent enough to read. The letterhead indicated that it was not from the judge but instead from the Cobb County DA's office. The letter was directed to my doctors, not me. Thankfully, one of the nurses was kind enough to let Sabrina keep it. Having worked with several suicidal patients before, she found the letter distasteful.

In addition to the hospital administration, copies were sent to all of my doctors and Dr. Warren, describing me as a dangerous criminal. Sabrina was smart enough to make a few calls and figure out just how many people had received this letter, which urged the staff to use "extra caution" in dealing with me, as if I posed a threat to them. The whole thing seemed ridiculous, especially given that I was staying in a mental hospital. Wasn't everyone in the mental hospital a danger in their own way? Isn't that why mental hospitals existed in the first place, to help mentally sick people heal?

Ever since the letter incident, the doctors who visited my bedside seemed a little more in a rush to move on to their next patient. The kind nurse had a new set of patients and many of the new nurses didn't even look me in the eyes when discussing my health. And even though Cobb County sent the letter to the medical staff, it didn't take long for the word to get out among the nurses that the new patient, Tyler, was some kind of financial criminal.

There was no point in trying to persuade the doctors and the new mental hospital therapist that I was not a criminal. The fact that I had been mixing with the Crips and Bloods in Cobb County was proof enough for them. My mother and Sabrina were not allowed to see me again after the initial visit when I'd regained consciousness. Even Shaun was denied the ability to see me. Surviving the suicide attempt felt to me like a kind of torture. I couldn't see any of the people who loved me and who I loved, who understood and believed what had happened to me. Plus, this place was even worse than a regular hospital. It was noisy, with random yelling and tantrums heard at all hours of the day. The air was frigidly cold, except for the rare moments when the AC would stop suddenly, at which point the room would become muggy with hospital odor. Many of the patients had gauze wrapped around their heads, and even more looked like walking zombies, totally dead in the eyes.

I had daily therapy, but it wasn't like it was with Dr. Warren.

This new therapist was more stoic but more aggressive at the same time. Our sessions felt more like an hour-long interrogation than an open opportunity to express my deepest feelings. He wrote on his clipboard more often than he made eye contact. And he often spoke in absolutes, which I really, really loathed.

My favorite part of the day was leisure hour, when I could choose to draw or play chess with one of the other patients. Usually, I sketched landscapes until my wrist started aching, but the cheap little pencil sharpeners were a nuisance. I'd rather be here than prison, don't get me wrong, but I was still getting used to the loneliness which I had to accept would follow me everywhere.

I craved kindness, if nothing more. That's where I looked to the nurses. They'd already been warned about me. But when they saw that I was polite, lonely, only wanting a bit of conversation to mix in with the injections and pills and blood samples, their professional demeanor kicked in. They smiled, nodded, shook their heads sympathetically when I told some of them, ones that seem genuine in their pity, about some of what I had gone through with Cindy and the DA. I don't know that any single nurse accepted what I told them. It was remarkable that their responses were so alike but never exactly the same.

"Just relax," is what the pleasant but dismissive nurse said.

"Don't think about that right now," said another, suggesting what I said is true but that it can't be changed.

"Just concentrate on getting better," advised another. When you tell a nurse that you've been framed for a violation that will put you away for the remainder of your life, how can they advise how a person gets "better" while living with that fact? Attaining justice would help, but even in the rare instance when a falsely accused prisoner is set free, is he ever completely healed? What medicine treats the lost years, the broken part of your soul that struggles to shout aloud, "How do I get those missing days and memories back?"

The nurses gave me warm, maternal advice. They sweetly pretended that they didn't think I was a criminal. And I enthusiastically acted like they were helping me. The only time this agreed-upon state of pleasant lying changed was when a doctor was nearby as well. Then, the nurse attended to her tasks, not interacting with the patient and, according to the physician, encouraging his criminal delusions.

I wondered, after I finally faced the court for sentencing, if anyone on staff in the mental hospital would take my side or at least show the slightest sympathy for me. It was, after all, a mental hospital. I hadn't attacked anyone. There must be a patient within these depressing, faded, spearmint-colored walls who had a much worse reputation than I did.

When I hobbled out into the activities room with the others, I ignored those who were curled up into balls or spoke only to themselves. I wondered about the patients who were aggressive, who swore, who, like possessive children, grabbed things from others. Surely, those patients were worse than me. They must have done things society would uniformly condemn.

The older man who had outbursts of anger directed against just about anyone in sight was a perfect example. How could he have gotten this far in life without being guilty of rape or murder or at the very least battering his poor old wife of many years over some trivial issue, like how she'd made runny mashed potatoes?

I began to wonder about the backstories of those in the mental hospital, how long they'd been there, what they had done, and so on. There was a teenaged girl who seemed very shy and spent time mostly by herself. I observed her sometimes while sharpening my pencils. It seemed like there were a lot of thoughts swimming around in her head. Eventually, I learned that her name was Monica after hearing one of the nurses address her as such.

I developed a rapport with one particular nurse, April, who always had a ready smile, her rounded, rosy cheeks suggesting she was always in a good mood. One day, I asked her about Monica, the young woman who spent little time with others and who occupied herself mostly by humming children's songs to herself and occasionally playing with dolls, although she seemed too old to be interested in them.

"April, it seems like such a shame that someone as young as Monica should wind up in here."

She nodded and complimented me. "There's a real goodness in you, Tyler. You care about other people, what they're going through. I like that about you."

"Thanks," I said and then cautiously continued, "I don't want to make you uncomfortable or anything, but do you know why Monica is here? She's so much younger than everyone else."

"Yes," April agreed, wanting to say more but working away instead.

I watched April for a few seconds. I softened my voice, making her stop to give me her full attention. "She should have had more of a break in life, you know?"

April looked deeply into my eyes and stopped changing the sheets on a patient's bed.

She thought a while and decided to trust me.

"All right, I'll tell you. I feel bad for her too. But you didn't hear this from me, okay?"

"Absolutely. Just between us."

April ducked her head quickly into the corridor and, seeing nobody, she delicately closed the door. "Monica grew up with a grandmother. Both of her parents had died. Monica worked around the house, did homework, never got to play with friends. It was like a Cinderella story, but without the prince. And the poor girl, she just lost her senses."

"What do you mean?" I asked.

"Her grandmother gave away the cat, the last connection to

Monica's parents. Monica picked up a hammer in the middle of the night and attacked her."

My eyes were wide open. "She hit her with a hammer? Did Monica kill her?" April returned to making up the bed. "That's all I know."

As the weeks dragged on, the doctors ordered that I take stronger medication than Dr. Warren had given me. I felt like I was always in a fog. I saw no reason for the drugs except to make me quiet, cooperative. I complained to the doctors first, which was a waste of time.

But I also knew that even if the nurses agreed with me about being over-medicated, there was nothing they could do without the authorization of one of the doctors in charge. Then, in addition to being groggy all the time, one of the pills they were forcing on me started to regularly give me headaches.

April was the only staff member who took pity on me. She couldn't change the medication I received, but she realized that because I was inactive all the time, I needed physical therapy to counterbalance the pills. So we started regular physical therapy sessions, where we'd walk around the park, or the doctor would watch me swim in the pool amongst the gaggle of old men wearing floaties on their arms.

The doctors weren't like April. They didn't like my being treated like a human being rather than a prisoner. They all had assumptions about me and they acted on those assumptions regularly. For example, just yesterday, I got into an altercation with a doctor over my physical state. I was feeling lightheaded after our walk, but when I explained the sensation to the doctor, he just replied, "Why would I trust anything you say? You probably just want drugs or special attention of some kind. We still have another lap to go. Let's see if you feel lightheaded when we get around that corner."

Physical therapy with April was much better, though, and my energy and attitude improved, despite being cut off from the outside world. I thanked April for helping me, and she gave me a brief but significant answer. As she passed by me, attending to her duties, April whispered, "It's up to you, now."

I thought about it and interpreted her meaning as controlling my own destiny as much as possible. To me, that meant finding a way of tricking the rest of the medical staff into thinking I was swallowing all of the pills they were constantly giving me.

It was a complicated process. First, I found an unused plastic bag in the kitchen and hid it under my mattress. Then, when a nurse gave me pills to take, instead of swallowing them, I tucked them under my tongue. I patiently waited until the nurse had left my room and then slipped the moist, still whole pill into the plastic bag and hid it again back under the mattress.

Late at night, when the nurses finished doing their rounds, I crushed the pills into a fine dust with a spoon and put it back into the plastic bag and hid it again. Then when they served mashed potatoes, which was almost every other day, I ate about half of them and mixed the powder from the pills into the rest of the potatoes.

What was I trying to accomplish by avoiding taking the pills? Clarity. And it worked!

I remembered more clearly what had actually happened between Cindy and me in our past when I stopped taking pills. Now, I believed that I could try to plan a way, somehow, out of my puzzle, out of the trap, by stopping my "medication" again. After all, if I didn't require the meds to stay alive, it was worth the chance to do some clear thinking and possibly come up with a good idea or two.

So, day after day, I got a bit stronger, through the exercises April had suggested for me. They assumed I was still popping their pills. I still kept to myself, and when I lay in bed, facing me on the wall was a photograph of a field of yellow flowers on a hillside. Hour after hour, I concentrated on that image, letting my now free mind wander, trying to find a way to get even with Cindy and prove my innocence.

The staff was happy because they were convinced I was withdrawing into myself. I was no longer running around asking questions and making demands. I wasn't causing a fuss over the pills. Instead, I was doing all of my work in my head, making connections and planning my next moves. To the doctors, I suddenly seemed introverted and relaxed. For them, they had successfully treated a criminal, even one who seemed innocent, by crushing his spirit.

Then, out of nowhere, the hospital announced that I was going to be released into police custody. I had ten minutes to collect my belongings and say my goodbyes, which I did in a haze, as I was still making connections in my mind. I decided my brain was a better place to live. Everything in the outside world was just an inconvenience, something I couldn't control, but in my head, I was free. I could travel anywhere and be anyone, so that's where I spent my time, even while I packed up my toothbrush and gave a nod to the little girl and her doll. I did try to see if there was anything I could do to postpone the inevitable. I asked if I would be able to spend time with my family, but the doctors said no, that it was a court decision and I was going directly to prison.

With my bags of belongings pinched between my fingers, two policemen escorted me out of the hospital in handcuffs, as if I was in a position to escape. My arms were limp when they locked the silver metal around my wrists. At some point, I had to accept that this was my reality. Instead of wasting energy trying to understand it, I wanted to focus on my solutions. How was I going to limit my time in prison? That's what I kept asking myself. I hardly noticed when the officer gave me a shove, pushing me toward the lobby like I was a horse that needed to be kicked into motion. I wasn't putting up a fight this time. I exchanged emotional glances with my mother, Sabrina and Shaun, who I didn't even know were there until I saw their melancholic faces in the lobby. We had just a matter of seconds to look at each other, not even enough time to wave. There was a definite, planned cruelty in how I was treated both at the hospital and when I was leaving it.

As they put me in the back of the police wagon and cuffed me to the walls, the officers must have been wondering why I was smiling. It was the memory of saying goodbye to April. The last thing I had said to her was whispered in her ear.

"Thank you for giving me courage, April. I have a plan now."

DESPITE ALL ODDS

Perhaps there is such a thing as being too forgiving. That's very cruel to say. It would be better if I said that whenever Cindy and I disagreed and she broke down in tears, I always forgave her, comforted her and never seemed to doubt her ability to make right the revelations she made. But sometimes, people take advantage of you when you're overly forgiving. And now, I realized, that was exactly my dynamic with Cindy. I had been thinking about Cindy a lot lately. Ever since I stopped taking the pills at the mental hospital, I didn't need my index cards to make sense of the relationship. I could remember everything perfectly, and I could observe it all from every angle.

I was still thinking about Cindy as I left the mental hospital. Although I had just said goodbye to my family, the final farewell before returning to prison, my mind was consumed with thoughts of my marriage—how it destroyed my life, and how I was going to get my life back. So as the police van thumped and tumbled along the streets, I ignored the stares of the guards. I avoided the past warm memories of my life and concentrated on Cindy, and how I might be able to reason with her. I had always given in to her. I had made the mistake of thinking that if I criticized anything about her or demanded to know what she was hiding from me, that our marriage would fall apart. Was that really true? Or was I cooperating in a game that made a fool out of me?

Cindy was strong-willed, suggesting that she had always had a backup plan if my suspicions got the better of me. She refused to even communicate with me. I sent forty-seven text messages in total, and left around twenty voicemails, but with each passing of the day, all I received was radio silence. Nothing. So what alternate plan did I have? And now, I knew that the deceit, the viciousness of James Marvin was behind her. Whether the plot was her idea or not, it was time to fully acknowledge that she was the kind of person you should not marry while she was cheating on you with a white pastor and district attorney.

As I went through the motions of returning to prison, I continued living life inside my head, grasping desperately for new insights, any new idea on how to get ahold of Cindy, so I could finally feel like I'd made some progress with my case. As I changed into my orange jumpsuit, I sounded out in my head what my next phone call would be like, and by the time I assembled my various belongings in my new cell, I had an outline of talking points for Cindy, if only I could get her to answer the phone. I knew that the voicemails were my best option. If I could penetrate her heart through one of my voicemails, maybe I could get her to call me back. It was not like I was acting, but I knew that in addition to the importance of the words, the emotion I used on those messages had to be real, convincing, or everything would be lost.

And that meant that something *in me* had to change. I had to seem different from the husband who was confused and frustrated by her actions. As I lay in my cell at night, after lights out, I thought to myself, "Cindy refuses to deal with me. She has Marvin to do her dirty work. How can I get her to make a small concession? Her position is to take everything, to give nothing."

What could I do differently that might change her behavior the slightest bit? The answer, strangely enough, occurred to me when I was in line with other inmates for food. The burly convict next to me was searching for something and didn't see it.

"Where's the Jell-O?" he demanded to know.

The inmate serving replied, "No Jell-O. It's pudding, man."

"They always got Jell-O!"

The inmate helping in the kitchen didn't hesitate with his response, "You want the pudding or not? Fuck, you think they're here to give us everything we want?"

The inmate took the pudding, disappointed, and the words echoed in my brain. *Everything we want.* Cindy approached my messages with the attitude of "You're going to give me everything I want." And why wouldn't she? Because I wrongly thought she had a conscience? She didn't.

The key to convincing her to visit me one time in prison, which I needed from her, was to show her that I was already defeated, that she and Marvin had already gotten what they wanted. Cindy needed to visualize her one journey to see me incarcerated as a final crushing victory for her, not a concession to a man she once loved and now was willing to see paralyzed. And that fact, that her willingness to see me absolutely humiliated, was the best hope I had for a plan that had no guarantee of success.

I waited as patiently as I could until the time when I could make an outgoing call. Since I used my first call to reach out to Mom and let her know I was settled, I had to wait two days before my next call. And every call after that, I would have to pay for, so I had to make this one count. While I waited, I thought about the words I had to say on her voicemail, but what was much more important, at that point, was the change in the tone of my voice. I could not sound threatening. I couldn't seem arrogant, like I had the upper hand, which I didn't. I had practiced alone, quietly, in my cell, trying to get the right intonation. Men by nature do not like to seem powerless in front of women, especially women they have been married to and certainly not women who have had their lover extort them.

I couldn't ask for advice from another inmate. *Excuse me? I'm going to give my wife everything in a divorce settlement. Do you think it sounds believable if I tell her like this...?* I know that there is a myth that crazy inmates get left alone, but I was new to the prison and didn't want to draw any extra attention.

I was next in line for the phone, running both the words and the feeling of the words through my head, as if they were being heard by Cindy. She had to be captured by something she heard that she hadn't before in my voice. If she hung up before the message was through, I would be doomed. There would be no hope at all. So I whispered to myself like one of the schizophrenics at the mental hospital while I waited in line for one of the four payphones lining the hallway. I was just beginning to repeat my speech again from the beginning when the guard announced I was up.

With shaky hands, I approached the phone and started dialing. As it rang, I took a deep breath. Then I was greeted by her familiar, recorded voice, unchanged and strong. It was up to me to lower myself, not exactly beg but to let her know that she was in control and that I knew that wasn't about to change.

"Cindy," I said, and I surprised myself because I heard my voice crack, simply saying her name. It was a phone message that could determine if I ever greeted the outside world again, one that could, if it failed, result in taking my own life, with no passerby with a cell phone to save me.

I cleared my throat gently. "Cindy. They took me from the mental hospital to prison. I-I can't stay in here for the rest of my life. So, I agree. I agree with what Marvin said. I sign the seventy-five thousand dollars over to you, and I won't fight you on the divorce. You can have everything. I'll enter a plea bargain and that's it. All I ask is that you bring the paperwork yourself. I'll sign it here and now, right in front of you. I just would like to know where we went wrong. Just tell me what I could have done differently. That's all. Could you do that for me? Just that?" I ended the call crying. I hung up.

The next guy in line, showing mercy in a hellish world, looked at the tears streaming down my face. "Hang in there," he said, uncomfortably.

I wiped the tears away briskly, and in my normal voice, I said to him, "Not a problem. It's all yours." I saw the confusion on his face and internally chuckled to myself. I decided that the difference between crying and acting like you're crying, if you're good at it, was that when you acted like you were crying, you could turn the tears off a lot quicker.

Cindy, again, did not contact me. But it was less than a week before I was told that John Marvin wanted to meet with me in an interrogation room at the prison. I wasn't sure if he was going to represent her in what he had to say or change the deal or what he was capable of doing. For the time being, I would have to present myself as I did on my call to Cindy: worn out, defeated, willing to give in to their demands.

As two guards escorted me toward the room, I wondered how many Black prisoners Marvin or his other prosecutors had extorted in the history of the county. But I also knew that I needed to play a part in order to accomplish anything, and whipping myself up into a righteous frenzy about racist DAs was not going to be helpful. I subtly slumped my shoulders in preparation for the ruthless threats that I'd soon be facing.

When the door was opened, I was a little surprised to see Marvin already there, with papers ready for signing. But I had no idea what they expected of me. I cast my eyes downward. Marvin nodded to the two guards, and they left the room, presumably standing right outside.

"Tyler, let me ask you something. If you were going to commit suicide, would it be such a big deal to sign that seventy-five thousand over to Cindy, like we asked?"

"Everything is different now," I said, not even raising my head. "How is it different?"

Should I assume that he and Cindy had already discussed each phone call? No. It would be more respectful to talk about her, as if Marvin was just overseeing things.

"I left a message with Cindy," I began. "I told her I couldn't go without seeing my family again on the outside. So, I agree to give her the seventy-five thousand and everything that will come out of the divorce."

"That's good to hear," Marvin said, "because we can enter a RICO sentence of thirty years, and the judge will sign off on it without a moment's hesitation."

"I know," I said.

Marvin looked over the papers he had brought me to sign. "So, you'll make things a lot easier on yourself by signing these papers."

But before he could lay the first agreement on the table and hand me the pen, I asked him, "Do you remember when I was surprised that you were a pastor? I didn't understand your thinking. I'm agreeing to the deal. I'm saying you are in charge. It's pointless to fight with you. All I wanted to know was why you're both a prosecutor and a pastor at a church. I mean, I'm confused. I'm a business owner. Why are you coming after me?"

Marvin sat down across from me and studied my drawn, miserable features. He smiled, as if the effort to explain things was pathetic but necessary, like the process of scolding a child who had done something obviously wrong. He was clearly enjoying the position he was in, both as an officer of the court and as a supposed teacher of wisdom.

"Tyler, you've done a couple of things wrong. First, you are guilty of stalking and threatening your wife. The punishment, based on your crime and your likelihood to commit it again, and your likelihood to commit that act with violence, is something that the prosecutor's office has the responsibility of dealing with."

He waited to see my reaction to that statement. "I understand that," I agreed.

Marvin nodded. "Okay. You get that. And in a wider sense, Tyler, you don't understand your place in society. If one of those Crip or Bloods thugs you've gotten to know in prison had attacked or robbed you, we have a certain responsibility to uphold the law.

"But all that has changed with Cindy. She's with me. You're no longer some middle-class, respectable Black citizen. You're another one of *them*. And you're going up against Cindy and me and the power of the office I represent. That's *your* position in this state and this society."

"I know that's the way it is, Mr. Marvin. It's why I'm going to sign over everything. I would just like Cindy to deliver the papers and tell me what went wrong between us. No matter what she says, I'll sign. All she has to do is tell me what she was thinking during our marriage."

Marvin thought about this change in direction. "What if she doesn't want to come?" he posed.

"Mr. Marvin, you and she get the seventy-five thousand and the divorce settlement. All I'm asking for is a one-time, face-to-face explanation, and she'll never have to see me again. Surely, you can convince her of that."

Marvin hesitated, rose, collected all of the papers and prepared to leave. "One meeting. That's it."

"That's all," I said.

"I think we can make that happen. I will be in touch."

He left, the door clanging shut behind me. I thought to myself,

We'll see how greedy Cindy is.

My socializing at the prison was not much different from my time at Cobb County Jail.

My plan was to keep to myself and discourage anyone from picking a fight with me. I figured it was less likely that any of the inmates in a major penitentiary would have heard about my being railroaded by Cobb County. First, there was not as much traffic going in and out of the prison. Second, prisoners came from all parts of the state, not just Cobb County.

And finally, I figured that long-time, hardened convicts would have little interest or sympathy for another case of a Black man being framed by the white establishment.

And that is why, in the afternoon after my second visit from Marvin, as I sat by myself, an inmate in the yard walked directly toward me, and I felt the pulse increase in my body. His eyes were completely focused on me. There was no mistaking that I was his target. I looked around the yard, seeing if the Black man in dreadlocks coming my way had any collaborators working with him. With a glance, I saw none, so I next looked around to identify the least crowded means of escape in the yard.

When I looked back, the inmate was yards from me. But he didn't seem as menacing, and I thought that if Marvin or a prison guard had ordered someone to eliminate me, this man with the dreadlocks and soft facial features didn't fit the bill. He looked more graceful now that he was closer. He wasn't stomping toward me but rather gliding with determination. He had a small piercing above his eyebrow, a gold hoop, and he was wearing a serious expression on his face… concern, maybe? Still, I was ready to prepare myself for a fight at the slightest move that suggested he was reaching for a knife.

Instead, he stopped a few yards short of where I sat and politely asked, "Is it okay if I join you?" Without waiting for a reply, he quickly added, "I have some information you'll be interested in." Then he took a pause. "About James Marvin."

He introduced himself as Rasta Doc. "Rasta because of the dreads. Doc because I'm always reading the newspapers in the library." I was still cautious and told him just my first name.

"I know who you are," he said confidently. "I heard from some guy at Cobb about you and Marvin and your wife. And I saw him earlier walking around and figured he was meeting with you." I said nothing. I was afraid of being labeled a snitch. And I still had no idea what Rasta Doc wanted. Rasta Doc reached inside a pocket of his jumpsuit. I stiffened, alert, worried.

"Man, take it easy. I told you, I read the papers all the time. And here's a little article I'm sure you're going to be fascinated by." He casually set down an article that had been ripped from a paper. I picked it up while Rasta Doc surveyed the yard, looking for potential trouble. The article was topped with a photo of Baron Krauss, newly elected a few months back as the governor of Georgia. In the picture, he was shaking hands with James Marvin. I looked up quickly at Rasta Doc.

"That's right," he said. "You don't have to read the article. I'll lay it out for you. Krauss gets elected, and what's the first thing he does? Puts his pal at the head of the racist Cobb DA in charge of the Georgia Bureau of Investigation. And your boy Marvin? Head of Cobb County DA, where he can continue to make money off of bullshit RICO cases. You see how it works around here? And Krauss is just straight evil, man. When he was secretary of state, he passed rules that prevented Black voter turnout. And it was the reason he barely beat the Black woman challenging him, Sonya Abraham. Now, Krauss has got others in Southern states taking away our rights to vote because they're afraid of being defeated."

I glanced over the rest of the article while replying, "No wonder my ex is so confident about ripping me off. She's connected to the racist power structure for the whole state of Georgia."

Rasta Doc rose. "You keep that clipping. Maybe it'll inspire you to get even with your ex-wife."

"And Rasta? Is there anything I can do to help you?"

"Me?" Rasta Doc chuckled, but it was in defeat. "They got me selling crack, and the sentence was like seven times more than selling the same amount of powder. Motherfucker Marvin and his gang got me in for thirty-five years."

I stood up and shook Rasta Doc's hand. "Thank you for this," I said.

"Good luck," he said in parting. "The odds are against you, but any revenge is better than nothing."

And then he nonchalantly disappeared into the yard of prisoners, with nowhere to go and all the time in the world to get there.

For me, the days stretched out agonizingly, with no progress, no contact from either Cindy or Marvin. After talking to Rasta Doc, I realized that the puzzle I was in was just another part of the history of the state. But, as it turned out, other prisoners, like Rasta Doc, felt a vengeful and violent association with Georgia's law enforcement and courts system.

A few days after my encounter with Rasta Doc, two large, intimidating, Black prisoners found me as I finished my meal by myself, as usual, in the cafeteria. They both sat down on either side of me.

"We want to talk. Rasta Doc told us about you, your ex-wife and James Marvin," said the first inmate. I decided now was not the time to mention that I never gave Rasta Doc permission to discuss my personal matters.

"What are you going to do about Marvin?" demanded the second inmate. "Are you going to take him out?"

"Me?" I said a little too quickly. I tried to sound reasonable without being cowardly. "I have no experience in this kind of thing."

"We do," said the first. "We both have life sentences for murder."

"We can help you hire professional hitmen to kill Marvin," said the second. My heart nearly skipped a beat. Did I hear them right? Life sentences for murder...yeah, I definitely heard them right. I saw a flash of Cindy's face in my mind, bloody and lifeless, and then my heart syncopated again.

"Marvin and my ex-wife are extorting me for all my money. I'm not the best person for this," I admitted.

I wondered for a moment if it were really that easy. If I could eliminate all of my problems with a simple "go-ahead." But I knew in my gut I couldn't be responsible for anyone's death, not even Cindy's. A shiver ran up my spine, but it wasn't cold outside.

The inmates looked at each other, obviously disappointed. They both rose, together.

"What about your ex-wife?" asked the second inmate. "She's behind this whole thing."

"I know," I admitted, embarrassed.

"I think," said the first, "that we could find someone to maybe kill her for free."

"I appreciate your help," I replied, "but if I did do that, I couldn't live with myself."

"Let us know if you change your mind," said the first inmate.

HOPE AFTER ALL

When sentencing in court finally arrived, I looked forward to and dreaded it at the same time. Of course, hearing the sentence read aloud by the judge would be real and final and undeniable, something that would make the nightmare a fact that I would live with, without much hope of correction. Taking a plea bargain, which I resisted for so long, made me look to the outside world like I was guilty. It didn't matter to most people, including those in the business world, that most cases never go to trial in the US. People, when innocent, often can't afford to fight injustice. And Cobb County was a prime example of the system being broken.

I also trusted the opinion of Cooper, who had little motivation as a public defender to actually help me. What if he exaggerated the willingness of the judge who would pronounce the sentence? And anything Marvin said was even more suspect. A prosecutor willing to throw a man's life away behind bars on a false charge could just as easily lie about lessening a jail sentence.

But I was out of options and knew that those people who mattered to me most believed that I was innocent, and that was some small comfort. I tried to keep that sentiment at the front of my mind as I stood in court for what felt like hours and hours, the cuffs pinching my wrists whenever I needed to fidget or adjust myself. Standing in court before the judge felt surreal. I had anticipated this day for so long and yet being here, standing in this experience as part of my current reality was like an out-of-body experience.

I constantly looked over at my mother and Sabrina. They were all seated together behind me, so I had to turn my head a good ninety degrees to see them. But I did so anyway just to exchange hopeful glances. Their supportive expressions distracted me from the lingering fear that this could all go terribly. Their expressions of concern, of love, even of fearfulness, gave me strength. Mom was already crying, which didn't surprise me.

Alternatively, I was so disgusted by what Cindy and Marvin had done to me that I found it difficult to look at them in court, even for a few moments. They were seated more in my line of vision, in the back left corner. Cindy had definitely just gotten her hair done. It was curled in a new fashion I had never seen before. She also had more eye makeup than usual, black all over her eyelids. If I didn't know to look for her, I may not have even recognized her. When we first made eye contact, I glared with my most venomous facial expression. Then I quickly looked away, avoiding her face for the remainder of the afternoon. It pained me to look at her. She was an absolute stranger now, and her new look confirmed it.

Then the judge peered down at us from on high, hardly giving me a glance. She studied the paperwork through her thin glasses, which were like oval slivers masking only her pupils. Her hands were veiny and fragile, peeking out of her black gown, but her expression was stern, and her body language was intimidating. She sat with her shoulders back, almost glued to the seat that resembled a throne. I watched as she analyzed the documents in front of her, although her mind had undoubtedly been made up, based on the recommendation of Marvin and the DA.

When it was her turn to address me, she asked me to rise and declared with a voice that was surprisingly deep given her tiny stature, "You were charged with one account of stalking on top of a RICO violation, is that correct, sir?"

I coughed. "That is correct, Your Honor." I felt better after hearing my voice for the first time, like I expelled some nerves through speaking out loud.

The whole courtroom thing still felt uncanny, like another universe. I felt that I was no longer in the United States but a parallel and much worse world.

As Cooper had instructed, I pleaded guilty, in a voice that suggested both fear and fury at the system I was unable to fight. The judge announced, after giving me a disinterested look, that I was to be sentenced to prison for seventeen years, not including the time I had already served. But that wasn't all. She also stated that I was responsible for $157,000 in restitution to Cindy. I didn't think I could be any more shocked than I was. But in addition to robbing me of $75,000 and my half of our estate, Cindy had managed to order me to pay even more money to her, money that I didn't have.

I quickly looked at Cooper, who hadn't even discussed the possibility of my being liable for restitution. He would not even meet my eyes. For Cooper, it was another case cleared off of a list. Of course he skipped mentioning restitution to me. It would have made it harder to convince me to plea bargain. I had just a few moments to look over at my family before the bailiff took me away.

With a final slap of the gavel, I was escorted out of the courtroom and led to my new sleeping destination. I didn't lift my head up the whole time, though, replaying today's events with each step forward. I hardly cared where I ended up at this point. The little bit of hope I once had was now gone. It could've been worse, I tried to remind myself, but even so, this restitution had my mind boggled. Where would I find all that money? When I finally looked up and took in my surroundings, I realized I had been taken to a prison that, to my horror, was even more terrifying than the jail where I had been sent to before. The cell I was assigned was visibly occupied with cockroaches. I saw two of them scurry under my bed as soon as I stepped foot in there.

I quickly realized that even if I killed many of them, there were always a few more to crawl over you at night when you were trying to sleep. To add to the suffering, the cell seemed particularly chosen for its hideous condition because it also had rats, though I didn't realize that until I tried to sleep that night. I heard them scurrying about, but I just thought it was some animal outside at first. Then, in the middle of the night, I felt the cold whip of one of their tails, and I nearly vomited right there, flinging it across the room like a reflex.

This continued throughout the night. I had to thrash my arms at them wildly when their rodent limbs got on top of me. As a result, I was always exhausted, sleep-deprived, feeling as if I had been placed inside an underworld of vermin and darkness and men shouting at and threatening to kill each other.

As an additional, final punishment, Marvin, using psychological torture, had the prison arrange to find a cell for me on the edge of that prison's death row. He must have figured that if he couldn't execute me, at least he could place me in sight of haggard, hardened men who had nothing to fear inside the prison walls, knowing their lives could be erased by the state at any given moment. Again, I was a model prisoner, speaking little, keeping to myself. This prompted a couple of different correctional officers to ask me why I had been given a cell in what was clearly the worst part of the prison.

Rather than tell them any part of my story, which would have made them scornful or even cruel in their treatment of me, I shrugged my shoulders and remained a question mark for them. Loneliness and alienation took over. I became desperate to talk to someone. I began to exchange brief nods or mumbled greetings to one of the

Black prisoners on death row. He seemed beaten down by life, not aggressive like most of the other inmates on the row.

Like me, he didn't seem to fraternize with the other prisoners. So, one day in the yard, spotting him sitting alone, I cautiously walked up to him and asked if I could talk with him.

His name was Claude, and although he seemed grateful to have me as company, he was less than willing to talk at first. So, as prisoners do, I began to tell him of my story, from suspecting Cindy of cheating on me to tripping on the rug and falling down the stairs, all the way to James Marvin's involvement with Cindy and his manipulating my case.

I gathered more passion, more anger and resentment, as I told Claude about the exceptional injustice of what had happened to me. It was as if I had stored everything up inside me for too long, and it all came tumbling out in front of a death row inmate who was ready and able to listen.

Finally, I concluded, stopping and studying Claude's face for a reaction but none came. Then, very gradually, he nodded a few times and said, in a deep, weary voice, "There are too many people who are in prison who were just in the wrong place at the wrong time. I ain't saying it's most people on the row or in this prison, but it's too many. And I'm one of them too."

I asked him to tell me his reason for being in prison. At first, Claude seemed hesitant.

He picked at his nails while he spoke in a hushed hurry, but at a certain point, his body relaxed. He made more eye contact, and something in him softened when he caught my gaze. Perhaps he recognized in me someone who cared and wanted to share the burden of a life destroyed by chance.

"People tell you a lot of things in here. Some true. Some not. But this is what went down and like you, it eats me from the inside out because it never should have happened. I was driving at night, near my home, rural county road. Like you, never had no record of anything. Out of nowhere, sheriff's car starts chasing me, lights on. I never did find out why. Was my taillight out? Did he even have a reason? So I pull over and hand him my license, and next thing, I see him sprinkle some rock in the backseat of my car."

"Cocaine?" I asked.

"Yeah. This guy wants me so bad, he's planting drugs on me. He gets the cuffs ready and tells me to get out of the car. I panicked and hit the gas. He started chasing me, and I was going fast. I knew the back roads and just had to get away. He took a sharp turn, trying to knock me off the road. Flipped his car, crashed into a tree. Dead. They caught me later. Gave me the death penalty. And I was just minding my own business. Like I say, there are people in here who done wrong. And there are people who just have the wrong color of skin."

Rather than making me feel like I had someone I could talk to, confide in, I felt even more alone after talking to Claude. It wasn't his fault. I believed his tale of drugs being planted on him. There was no glory in his story. It didn't seem like the kind of lie an inmate created or changed in order to impress another. And Claude's whole attitude, his general personality of defeat, made him more believable. It also made me more hopeless about ever finding a way back into the outside world. I grew more depressed, ate less, exercised little, and when I called Sabrina, I found it difficult to talk.

She told me about her efforts to find representation, find Thomas Drew, find any lead that might shine a ray of light on my case. Sabrina was working as hard as any private investigator. It was just that there was no progress. The years of my sentence stretched out before me in my mind. If I had to serve the full seventeen years, what would greet me when I entered back into society? Would my mother still be alive? Would Sabrina or Shaun still want to have any kind of relationship with me?

And in addition to those fears, I would still be liable to pay Cindy $157,000, after she and Marvin already extorted money out of me. The thought of that made the blood pump angrily through me, and I was filled with visions of violence and retribution that I struggled to remove from my mind.

But I reminded myself that my anger meant that I felt there was a chance, no matter how slim, to gain some justice in my case. Claude was a broken man. He had no more hopes. It was clear that he believed in one of two options for himself: One, he would be sentenced to death. Or two, Claude would wither away in the prison hospital, with no visitors to distract him, or give him courage, as his health became worse and worse.

The darkness I felt in that prison was so deep that when I next called Sabrina, I didn't recognize at first that she sounded optimistic and energetic.

"I got in touch with this Black attorney, Tate Jefferson. He's with the federal court in Fulton County." There was a pause. Sabrina had mentioned other lawyers in the Atlanta area who might have helped. Each time, the more they heard about my case, the easier it was for them to decide not to get involved.

"Ty?"

"What?"

"This guy is what we've been looking for. A friend of his at the Georgia Bar Association told Tate about the audiotape you made of Cooper. And the agreement from Cindy and Marvin that I made copies of. He said he wants to see everything. Isn't that great?"

I tried to sound positive, but inside, part of me had no expectation that an outside attorney would, or even *could,* take on Cobb County.

"I hope he helps us," I said. I couldn't prevent some desperation creeping into my voice.

"I've already mailed the materials to him," Sabrina stated. Then, she became wary.

"Ty, what's wrong? We have a good chance of getting him to help."

I took a quick look around at the other inmates, waiting to use the phone. How many of them had plans to appeal their convictions? And how many years did they continue their efforts before giving up?

"Never mind. I'm just not feeling well. You've done a great job, no matter what happens."

"I'm telling you," Sabrina insisted, her toughness coming across the other end of the telephone line. "This guy wants to help. You'll see."

"Okay," I replied and made an effort to sound more positive. "So, if he's interested, the next step is you and him coming down here to meet face to face."

Sabrina agreed. I thanked her and told her that I loved her. I hung up, hating myself for pretending to be optimistic and at the same time, feeling that Tate Jefferson might be my only chance at freedom, and I didn't like the odds.

My mood was being yanked this way and that when I found out that Tate Jefferson wanted to have a meeting and was willing to drive over from Fulton County to do so. I wondered if he was willing to take on James Marvin as well as Cindy, if he had to get permission from others above him, if it would cost a great deal and if I would be able to afford it.

Judging by his appearance, Tate Jefferson was definitely more than I could easily afford. One look told you that he was another class from Cobb County prosecutors, from his designer suit and Italian shoes to the alligator-hide briefcase he dove into, pulling documents out and lining them up for discussion.

In the visitors' area, alongside us, Sabrina smiled expectantly. I carefully judged everything about Tate, from his tall, lean body to the way his gold-rimmed glasses stood out on his shaven head and how focused he was when he finally finished unpacking his briefcase, turning his full attention to me.

Tate surprised me, starting off by saying how sorry he was for my false incarceration.

Then he systematically went over the evidence Sabrina had provided. After I confirmed everything, he smiled and looked over at Sabrina.

"Sabrina, it turns out," Tate said pleasantly, "is a very fine detective. Do you want to tell him?"

There was a pause. "Tell me what?" I said impatiently.

Sabrina drew her chair in and lowered her voice. "Thomas Drew," she said. "I found him."

"I put my PI on it," Tate added, "and in fact, we confirmed where Drew lives and works. Sabrina explained to me why he's important to the case. Briefly, Tyler, tell me what you were thinking regarding Thomas Drew."

"I believe that my ex, Cindy, gave herpes to Drew, who threatened her. If we can get him to go public and officially name her, as a doctor who knowingly passed on an STD, it will put pressure on the hospital. We can go after her medical license and hopefully tie this in with her relationship with Marvin." I stopped, hoping he agreed with my tactics.

"It's going to be difficult going after Marvin, with his support from the governor and others," Tate began. I threw my hands up in the air, frustrated.

"Wait," Tate added. "Wait a minute. I agree with you that the more pressure we put on Cindy, and by association Marvin, the better our chances to drive a wedge between them.

Also, I can file motions about wrongful incarceration that can get your conditions improved while we continue the fight."

I breathed out. For the first time, I saw a strategy that might work and an attorney that could make it happen.

"All right, Tate. I like the sound of this. I'm being ripped off by

Cindy and Marvin, but I still have enough money to cover Drew's expenses to file against Cindy and the hospital."

Sabrina jumped in. "I discussed this a bit with Tate," she said proudly. "He said he's willing to defer his fees for now."

I whipped my head in the direction of Tate, looking for confirmation.

"The federal court in Fulton County is investigating not only your ex-wife but Cobb County's DA. As for any expenses I personally incur on your behalf, I'm willing to discuss a fair payment schedule with you...down the road."

It was more than I'd hoped for. And even though success was far from guaranteed, I let out a little chuckle. "Thank you, Tate. Thank you. I just hope you don't have to wait seventeen years for me to pay you."

Tate began putting everything back in his briefcase. "If we do this right, you're not going to have to wait seventeen years." He looked at both me and Sabrina. "But it's going to take patience and hard work. We can put a lot more pressure on Cindy than we can on James Marvin. But what we find out about Cindy, even without proof regarding her involvement with Marvin, will strengthen your case."

Tate stood, and Sabrina and I joined him. Sabrina beamed. I knew what she was going to say and smiled right back at her.

"I told you," Sabrina boasted proudly. "I found our guy."

"You did. Thank you both for believing in me." Sabrina waved off my compliment.

Tate grabbed his briefcase. "So, my emails and phone calls will go through Sabrina if you need quick updates and then official documents will be sent to you, Tyler, as well as copies for you, Sabrina, at your business office. First thing, I'm going to pay Thomas Drew a surprise visit, and if you're right about him, file a complaint against Cindy and the hospital."

"Great," I agreed. Tate paused. "Sabrina tells me they've put you in a filthy cell, facing death row. Is this true?"

"It is," I said.

"Well, we're going to change that pretty damn quick."

After the meeting with Sabrina and Tate, despite the uncertainty, I felt energized. I had to admit, this was the first attorney I'd met who seemed confident, *really* confident. And that confidence was infectious. By now, I had already learned the importance of maintaining low expectations, but I couldn't help the blood rushing to my cheeks, the corners of my lips rising at the thought of getting a better cell. Maybe...just maybe I had hope after all. But I slapped my face to remind myself nothing was certain yet. This was good news, but I needed to stay realistic, stay humble. I knew Sabrina would immediately notify the rest of our family about the news. There was only one person I wanted to share the information with.

But as the guard escorted me back, I saw that Claude was no longer in his cell. He had been replaced by another Black prisoner. I looked back at the guard. "Please. Can I just ask this guy one question?" The guard responded by marching me along quicker, without a reply.

When I got a few feet in front of the cell, I shouted, "What happened to Claude, the guy who was in this cell?"

The inmate in Claude's former cell shrugged his shoulders, but the prisoner in the cell next door shouted back at me, "They gave him the needle! Three days ago!"

I slumped, as if punched in the stomach. I suddenly had no air. The guard opened my cell. I lay down and curled into a ball as the door clanged shut.

A REAL-LIFE MIRACLE

As crushed as I felt when I learned that Claude had been executed, I held onto the hope that Tate Jefferson would make progress with my case. Even though Claude was no longer among the inmates, just the presence of death row reminded me of Claude's haunting story. His wrongful conviction for an incident that could have been avoided made me wish I'd spent more time talking with him.

Neither one of us socialized with other inmates, and the kinship I felt with him actually grew despite his being gone. There was something ironic about my conversation with Claude. It was so filled with defeat and depression, but it happened around the same time that Sabrina and I met with Tate at the prison and made plans for my case.

Tate's parting words when we saw each other were a promise to address the hideous cell that I'd been given. And one day, barely a week after that meeting, a guard showed up at my cell and announced that I was going to be "relocated."

I certainly didn't question the guard as to why the prison

suddenly realized the error of its decision. Instead, I gathered my belongings quickly and followed the guard to a new block, where I was given a cell without vermin. And it was not in view of death row, which had been prompting the painful memory of Claude's execution, every day.

I didn't know how much Tate would be able to accomplish in the end, regarding our plans, but at the very least, I was impressed that he'd put pressure on someone that led so quickly to my being placed in a better cell. He must have been in contact with Cobb County. I would have loved to have seen the expression on Marvin's face when he learned a federal prosecutor in Atlanta was aware of the Cobb County DA's corruption and was fighting for better treatment for me.

I was looking forward to discussing the recent news with Sabrina, as I waited to make a phone call to her from within the prison. As it turned out, Sabrina was more informed about the latest details regarding Tate's accomplishments.

"Tate notified me. I'm so glad. Now, you'll finally be able to sleep better."

I agreed. "We have a long way to go, but he's clearly letting the Cobb County prosecutors know he's on the case."

Sabrina's voice became higher and took on more energy. "And I have some news for you. Tate just let me know earlier today."

"Okay. What?"

"I'll give you a big hint. You're a genius. And I am a great private eye."

"Thomas Drew?" I guessed, my excitement growing. "Did he confirm he had contact with Cindy and got herpes? Is he going to cooperate with us?"

"He's already cooperated, Ty. Papers have been served against the hospital, saying that there will not be a lawsuit against the hospital if they test Cindy for STDs, and if she tests positive, they fire her."

I had to think a few moments about this. "Tate is really doing great work for us. If the hospital fires Cindy, there might be a way to turn her against Marvin."

"Have patience," Sabrina said. "Tate said that the idea of removing Marvin from office is going to be tough. He's going to deny any relationship with Cindy to protect himself. But Ty, we have a real chance now to portray Cindy's testimony as lies. And that can only help your case, your sentence."

"You're right again, as usual...detective," I said to her, my mood suddenly and dramatically improved.

I was very appreciative of the work Tate had done so far on my behalf and scheduled a phone call with him to discuss tactics, but before I could speak with him in his Atlanta office, I received from him a photocopy of an official record from the court. I couldn't entirely understand it, but there was language in the document mentioning my transfer to another location.

When I finally reached him on the phone, Tate was in good spirits. He explained the transfer document.

"I petitioned the Cobb County DA to send me their records on the charges against you. I had to ask twice, and I see why they delayed. The charges on the stalking are very weak and the RICO violation is totally unsupportable. I can't get them to vacate the conviction, not yet anyway, but the paperwork you see is an order to transfer you to a 'halfway house' in Cobb County. I'll still be working on the case, but meanwhile, you'll be living in a home-like environment with other nonviolent offenders. And Tyler, it will be much easier for you to have family and friends visit you there."

"This is wonderful," I exclaimed and got choked up, unable to speak.

"You still there?" Tate asked.

"I'm still here," I managed to hoarsely say. "Thank you, Tate. It'll mean so much to see my family after all this time."

"I'm sure it will," Tate said. "Meanwhile, we're waiting to see what Cindy's hospital is going to do about testing her. Personally, I feel like they'll agree to it. They don't want the publicity of fighting our office if they can avoid it by simply administering a test."

"Right, but what if the test comes out negative? We probably can't make Cindy take more than one test, right?"

"No," Tate admitted, "but let's be hopeful about things. And meanwhile, prepare to have your own room in a house in Marietta that's a lot nicer than the place you're staying now."

The Marietta Recovery House was a compact but pleasant-looking house on the outskirts of town. The staff and the residents were an entire world apart from what I had just experienced in the prison settings. The men were nonviolent offenders, convicted for first-time offenses like minor drug possession. They were not difficult to talk to. From the moment I stepped into the lobby, I knew this living situation would prove a major upgrade. The lobby alone had a cozy feeling to it, despite it being a halfway house. It had a watercooler in the corner and tan shag carpet, ivory walls with a white chair rail and warm lighting...

Something about it felt almost homey. It wasn't until then that I realized just how deprived I'd been of that homey essence.

As for the staff members at Marietta Recovery House, they were clearly trained to not tolerate breaking rules of the house. But on the other hand, you could talk with them, ask questions, even trade stories about those you had met in the penal system. Each resident of the house was given chores around the place and the manager of the house, Reuben, conducted group meetings and discussion sessions, and oversaw the staff and made sure that each resident fulfilled his assignment.

Reuben was the one who greeted me when I first arrived. I must have looked confused because he took one look at me and asked, "You new here?"

"Yes," I admitted.

"I'm Reuben," he reached out his hand for me to shake it. I couldn't help but smile slightly at the friendly gesture. This certainly wasn't Cobb County Correctional.

"I'm Tyler," I replied.

"I'll show you to your room. I suspect you understand the basic ground rules. No violence, no funny business. This isn't prison, and I expect everyone to behave themselves with a certain level of respect."

"I'm just so happy to be here." The words blurted out of me before I could even think about what I was saying.

Reuben squeezed my shoulder. "Life gets better, man. You're in a better place now."

I smiled fully, teeth and all, as he led me to my room at the end of the hall.

The schedule at the House was set firmly, although life, interaction, even the food was a marked improvement over what I had experienced of late. After dinner, those who were assigned to the halfway house could receive brief, five-minute phone calls of importance.

Reuben, one evening, a few weeks after my arrival, peeked his head into my small dormitory-like room. When he saw me, he wedged his wide shoulders in as well.

"Tyler, phone call for you. You know the drill: five minutes, max."

I thanked him, walked to the end of the upstairs hallway and sat down in an overstuffed armchair next to a small table and telephone. It was Sabrina, and her words rushed out like a torrent of water as soon as I said hello. "Ty, I know I only have five minutes, but this is a day we've been waiting for. Tate just called and said that Cindy's hospital came back with a positive test for herpes. And she was so stressed that she made an error while performing an operation on a patient. So, she is being sued for the medical error and the hospital has fired her."

I was confused, not by the news but by the question of how to feel. Certainly, there was some justice in her being punished, and it might help Tate with my case, but it was also Cindy, someone I had once loved. I felt foolish that I hadn't sensed what she would do to me and, as it turned out, Thomas Drew and possibly others.

"That's amazing," I managed to say. "Do you know if she'll still be able to practice medicine?"

"I doubt it," Sabrina said with assurance. "Tate made the state medical board aware of her firing, and they told him that once they get confirmation from the hospital, she'll lose her medical license for Georgia."

We had done it. We'd exacted some level of revenge against Cindy, although there was still a wrongful conviction against me on the record.

"Great news," I told Sabrina. "Give Tate my thanks until I can talk with him myself.

And I'm going to see if they'll let me have a small celebration over here with you guys."

Reuben, after I told him what I had learned, smiled widely. He was immediately on my side, even though I had seen my family once when I first arrived at the house. Reuben arranged for my mother, Sabrina and Shaun to come over on a Sunday afternoon for cake, soda, coffee and other snacks. My family met the staff and residents briefly, and then we were given privacy for our little party in the front room of the house. My mother and Shaun asked questions about my case, questions that I didn't want to dwell on and in fact, questions I couldn't answer yet.

I prompted Shaun to tell me about his life. He mumbled some generalities, and when I pressed him for more details, he said, "Dad, can I talk with you for a few minutes, just you and me?" He turned to Sabrina and his grandmother and repeated, politely, "Just for a few minutes?" I saw nothing but love and encouragement on the faces of Sabrina and my mother. I put an arm around Shaun's shoulders and we walked out onto the front porch of the house.

We stood a while in silence, observing the town where we had both grown up. Finally, Shaun spoke. "Dad, I'm sorry."

I was puzzled. "*I* should be apologizing. You probably have had friends who've said some cruel things to you about me."

"No, that–that happened, but it doesn't matter. What matters is I doubted you. I didn't know what was true and what wasn't, and I should have written to you in prison. But now I know what's been going on, and it's been terrible for you. And I promise, I won't doubt you again."

We hugged each other hard. I breathed a huge sigh. "Shaun, thank you. I don't blame you for any of that."

His eyes widened a bit, relieved. "Really?"

"No," I said. "I don't blame you at all. What's important is how we feel *now*. And I'm telling you, knowing you believe me, and believe in me, is what it's all about."

Cindy, for all of her lying and destructiveness, had been punished. It was going to be impossible for her to practice medicine anymore. Other men came forward and filed suit against her for giving them herpes. What we proved would affect my standing in the community. Tate had already gotten remarkable results. There was no disputing that.

Cindy had enough to worry about, with legal issues regarding her former practice and her new state of unemployment. I wasn't worried about her trying to personally continue to go after me.

I knew Marvin was powerful and as aggressive and corrupt as Cindy was, so I was surprised when I got my next phone call at the Marietta Recovery House. I learned that Tate had accomplished even more in his investigation of my case and how the Cobb County DA was being run.

"It's obvious that you want to get even with Marvin," Tate insisted on the phone call. "I can't immediately get rid of Marvin, as much as we both would like that. What I have discovered, though, is the connection between him, the governor and the head of the GBI. I want to let him know that we realize their corruption using you and the RICO charges. And I've found other RICO cases that they illegally used to extort money from other Black defendants. I want to serve him notice that we're going to be coming after Marvin and his buddies who promoted him."

I was so amazed that I found it hard to speak. "So, we might be able to make the evidence public and affect the chances of the governor being elected in the next election?"

"Yes. The way I see it," Tate said slowly, "if we get rid of the governor, we don't have to deal with his dirty government appointees anymore. I'll meet with Marvin in a restaurant down there. I told him I have information I want to talk to him about regarding his relationship with Cindy, and Marvin agreed to meet. But when we finally do, I'll throw everything at him: DA records, arrest reports, the extortion attempt he and Cindy made. Everything. Sabrina even got some smaller newspapers to cover your case and raise questions about your conviction."

"Okay," I agreed, although I was both nervous and excited about the potential outcome.

"You've got to understand one thing, Tyler. We're going all out with this nuclear attack on Marvin. The idea is to intimidate him, to make him wonder if the governor will only protect himself. While the federal court is doing its job to make everyone aware of the corruption, with a little luck, under pressure, these guys will turn on each other and the first one in will get a plea bargain."

I thought about this scenario. "Would it help if you made Marvin question whether Cindy, in desperation, could be turned against him? After all, she's really unstable and desperate right now."

"It's a good thought," Tate acknowledged. "We've got to throw everything we can at him."

"I want to be there," I insisted. "I can get the manager of the house, Reuben, to allow me to go out with my attorney for lunch. I want to see Marvin's face, the look in his eyes."

Tate paused a while on the phone. "Your being there could help. But you have to promise me one thing."

"What?"

"Don't say a single word until I get him, then and there, to sign an agreement I'm going to draw up. Can you promise me that?"

I smiled. "Tate, after everything you've done for me, that's the least I can do."

~

In the restaurant Marvin agreed to meet Tate at, he walked in with a general air of overconfidence. Tate stood and shook his hand. They both sat down at the table, and that's when I strolled over from the bar and sat down with them. Marvin stuttered out a protest. Tate interrupted him, forcefully putting on the table each piece of evidence as he mentioned it.

"Mr. Marvin, I'm filing the following evidence against you in federal court. A recording featuring one of your public defenders, Cooper, telling my client that RICO violations are used to extort money regularly from defendants. Speaking of RICO, court records I obtained about the federal charges that are so weak, I immediately got him released from a major penitentiary, next to the death row block, to a halfway house for nonviolent offenders. Also, the stalking charges used against my client to take all marital assets was unsupported. Records of your personal visits to my client, while he was imprisoned, including your document on behalf of his ex-wife, Cindy, with whom you were having an extramarital affair, attempting to extort seventy-five thousand dollars from my client—"

"Listen, you think—"

"I'm not done with the evidence," Tate said, cutting off Marvin. "This same document was presented by my client's ex-wife, and we have the original document she gave him, in addition to her verbal admission of the affair with you and, of course, record of her prison visit to my client. By the way, you may have heard, my client's ex-wife, who was a member of your church where you are a pastor, was recently fired by her hospital as a doctor who had spread a sexually transmitted disease to one Thomas Drew. She has recently been stripped of her medical license and sued for malpractice."

Tate let the pile of evidence sit on the restaurant table for a few moments. "Now, Mr. Marvin, my office is ready to oversee a civil suit filed against my client's ex-wife. We can wipe her out financially, or we can allow her to plea bargain, in exchange for testifying against you. You think she won't flip? In fact, since losing her medical practice, I'm willing to bet you don't take her calls anymore."

Marvin looked over at me, expecting me to say something. I merely bore into his eyes, my anger and disgust obvious and intense. This gave Tate time to add to the growing heap on the table. He tossed down two newspaper stories about my case, with Marvin's name highlighted in each one.

"Here's local coverage of this case, including questions about your office. Our office can make this story go national, and bring in your good friends the governor and head of the Georgia Bureau of Investigation."

"I've heard enough!" Marvin angrily announced. Tate and I waited to see what he next said. His voice was a low growl. "What do you want?"

And then I saw a side of Tate I had never seen. He leaned over toward Marvin and looked like he was going to strike him. "I want you to let your friends, the governor and the head of the GBI know we are going after all three of you. You're looking at charges that include the false imprisonment of my client. You may want to consider cooperating with us before your buddies try and put the blame entirely on your corrupt, racist fucking ass." Marvin raised his eyebrows in surprise.

As Marvin rose, Tate, now relaxed, said, "Anything you want to add, Tyler?"

"Yeah," I replied. "Marvin, you better get tested for STDs. Cindy probably gave you herpes too."

~

We celebrated my freedom and the legal victory over James Marvin by inviting Tate Jefferson down to Marietta. Sabrina and I made a lavish, home-cooked meal for everyone.

While we were relaxing over carrot cake and coffee, I pulled out my collection of three-by-five notecards. I explained to Tate how despite the injury to my head and the medications that were jumbling my mind, the memories I jotted down on those cards made me hopeful, gave me insight and sometimes helped me solve portions of the puzzle that had unexpectedly taken over my life.

"I wish I could write a memoir about all this," I said, thumbing through the cards, the scattered but powerful memories.

Tate smiled as he finished another forkful of carrot cake. "I got you the best deal I could. If you wrote a non-fiction book, you'd just be inviting Marvin, the head of the GBI and the governor to come after you on another charge, at this point."

"He's right," Sabrina said. "Even with two years in jail and fifteen years of probation, it's a miracle Tate got you out."

"Of course, we might just stir up enough controversy to get the governor voted out in the midterms. That is a distinct possibility."

"It is," I agreed, "but if he gets re-elected, and I can't write a memoir, I just wish there was another way to let people know what goes on down here."

“There is,” Tate declared, cleaning the frosting off of his fork. “Write a novel and change the names.” I chuckled as I dabbed at my mouth with a napkin.

I didn’t respond, but instead, I took in the words as I glanced at the faces around me. Tate was stuffing carrot cake into his mouth with increasing speed, and Sabrina was twirling her hair, a permanent smile etched on her face. As I took in the present moment, a warmth filled my chest like the sensation which follows the first sip of champagne, or a first declaration of love from a significant crush. I had attended Sunday mass every week for over thirty years, but sitting here, eating cake with scars collaged across my body, I felt the presence of God like I never had before.

Finally, I understood what it meant to experience a real-life miracle. To exist on the right side of justice. I’d been to hell and back, but right now, here in this squeaky wooden chair among smiling faces, I had found heaven on Earth. I could stay right here forever.

AFTERWORD

Racism is an ongoing problem in America but becomes especially apparent in our judicial system. Black men are incarcerated at a rate nearly five times that of whites. They are more likely to experience delays in hearings and trials, inexperienced attorneys, police brutality or inaccurate crime scene processing, extended or inappropriate sentencing, and even false imprisonment.

While this story is fictitious, that doesn't detract from the fact that this is a real problem and happens every day in America. The greatest country on Earth still operates on outdated, racist systems that unjustly violate the rights of Black Americans.

Tyler's story isn't just about justice and revenge, though. It is also about the strength of the human spirit. When faced with life-changing charges, Tyler fought back. He refused to become another statistic. He sought the truth not just for himself but in hopes that one day all Black Americans could expect true justice as well.

Taree Brown is an entrepreneur, actor, philanthropist and founder of Above the Obstacle Foundation, which provides affordable housing for low-income individuals, the disabled, and senior citizens.

Originally from Louisiana, he spent his adult life in Georgia and now lives in California. *Intense Lies* is Taree's first book and chronicles his own experiences of being wrongfully accused, imprisoned and, ultimately, freed. He hopes the book serves as an inspiration of persistence and faith.

Made in the USA
Columbia, SC
07 September 2022

66159789R00117